THE BIG BLUE SOLDIER

THE BIG BLUE SOLDIER

BY

GRACE LIVINGSTON HILL

[MRS. LUTZ]

AUTHOR OF "THE CITY OF FIRE," "MARCIA SCHUYLER," ETC.

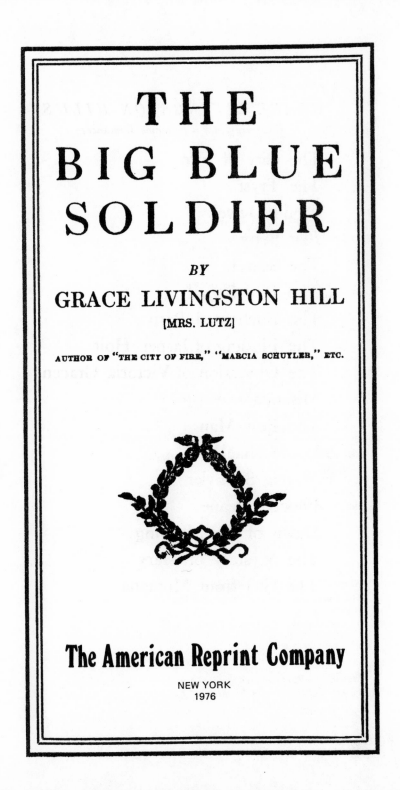

The American Reprint Company

NEW YORK
1976

Republished 1976 by Special Arrangement
with J.B. Lippincott Company

Copyright © 1920, 1921 by The Golden Rule Company
Copyright © 1923 by J.B. Lippincott Company

Library of Congress Cataloging in Publication Data

Hill, Grace Livingston, 1865-1947.
    The big blue soldier.

    Reprint of the ed. published by Lippincott, Phil-
adelphia.
    I. Title.
PZ3.H55Bi7   [PS3515.I486]   813'.5'2   75-46602
ISBN 0-89190-002-0

AMERICAN REPRINT, a division of
The American Reprint Co./Rivercity Press
Box 476
Jackson Heights, New York 11372

*Manufactured in the United States of America
by Inter-Collegiate Press, Inc. Mission, Kansas*

THE BIG BLUE SOLDIER

CHAPTER I

"AND you don't think maybe I ought to have had lemon custard to go with the pumpkin instead of the mince?"

Miss Marilla Chadwick turned from her anxious watching at the kitchen window to search Mary Amber's clear young eyes for the truth, the whole truth, and nothing but the truth.

"Oh, no, I think mince is much better. All men like mince-pie, it's so—sort of comprehensive, you know."

Miss Marilla turned back to her window, satisfied.

"Well, now, if he came on that train, he ought to be in sight around the bend of the road in about three minutes," she said tensely. "I've timed it often when

5

folks were coming out from town, and it always takes just six minutes to get around the bend of the road."

All through the months of the Great War Miss Marilla had knit and bandaged and emergencied and canteened with an eager, wistful look in her dreamy gray eyes, and many a sweater had gone to some needy lad with the little thrilling remark as she handed it over to the committee:

"I keep thinking, what if my nephew Dick should be needing one, and this just come along in time?"

But when the war was over, and most people had begun to use pink and blue wool on their needles, or else cast them aside altogether and tried to forget there ever had been such a thing as war, and the price of turkeys had gone up so high that people forgot to be thankful the war was over, Miss Marilla still held that wistful look in her eyes, and still spoke of her nephew Dick with bated breath and a sigh. For was not Dick among those favored few who were to remain and do patrol work for an indefinite time in the land of the enemy, while others were gathered to their waiting homes and eager loved ones? Miss Marilla spoke of Dick as of one who still lingered on the border-land of terror, and who laid his young life a continuous sacrifice for the good of the great world.

A neat paragraph to that effect appeared in *The Springhaven Chronicle,* a local sheet that offered scant news items and fat platitudes at an ever-increasing rate to a gullible and conceited populace, who supported it because it was really the only way to know what one's neighbors were doing. The paragraph was the reluctant work of Mary Amber, the young girl who lived next door to Miss Marilla and had been her devoted

friend since the age of four, when Miss
Marilla used to bake sugar cookies for
her in the form of stogy men with currant eyes and outstretched arms.

Mary Amber remembered Nephew
Dick as a young imp of nine who made
a whole long, beautiful summer ugly
with his torments. She also knew that
the neighbors all round about had memories of that summer when Dick's
parents went on a Western trip and left
him with his Aunt Marilla. Mary
Amber shrank from exposing her dear
friend to the criticisms of such of the
readers of *The Springhaven Chronicle*
as had memories of their cats tortured,
their chickens chased, their flower-beds
trampled, their children bullied, and
their windows broken by the youthful Dick.

But time had softened the memories
of that fateful summer in Miss Marilla's
mind, and, besides, she was sorely in

need of a hero. Mary Amber had not
the heart to refuse to write the paragraph, but she made it as conservative as
the circumstances allowed.

But now, at last, among the latest to
be sent back, Lieutenant Richard
Chadwick's division was coming home!

Miss Marilla read in the paper what
day they would sail, and that they were
expected to arrive not later than the
twenty-ninth; and, as she read, she con-
ceived a wild and daring plan. Why
should not she have a real, live hero herself? A bit belated, of course, but all
the more distinguished for that. And
why should not Mary Amber have a
whole devoted soldier boy of her own for
the village to see and admire? Not that
she told Mary Amber that, oh, no! But
in her mind's vision she saw herself,
Mary Amber, and Dick all going together to church on Sunday morning,
the bars on his uniform gleaming like

the light in Mary Amber's hazel eyes. Miss Marilla had one sudden pang of fear when she thought that perhaps he would not wear his uniform home, now that everybody else was in citizen's clothing; then her sweet faith in the wholesomeness of all things came to her rescue, and she smiled in relief. Of course he would wear it to come home; that would be too outrageous not to, when he had been a hero. Of course he would wear it the first few days. And that was a good reason why she must invite him at once to visit her instead of waiting until he had been to his home and been demobilized. She *must* have him in his uniform. She wanted the glory of it for her own brief share in that great time of uplifting and sacrifice that was so fast going into history.

So Miss Marilla had hastened into the city to consult a friend who worked in the Red Cross and went out often to the wharves to meet the incoming boats. This friend promised to find out just when Dick's division was to land, to hunt him up herself, and to see that he had the invitation at once. "See that he *came*," she put it, with a wise reservation in her heart that the dear, loving soul should not be disappointed.

And now, the very night before, this friend had called Miss Marilla on the telephone to say that she had information that Dick's ship would dock at eight in the morning. It would probably be afternoon before he could get out to Springhaven; so she had better arrange to have dinner about half past five. So Miss Marilla, with shining eyes and heart that throbbed like a young girl's, had thrown her cape over her shoulders and hastened in the twilight through the hedge to tell Mary Amber.

Mary Amber, trying to conceal her inward doubts, had congratulated Miss

Marilla and promised to come over the first thing in the morning to help get dinner. Promised also, after much urging, almost with tears on the part of Miss Marilla, to stay and help eat the dinner afterward in company with Miss Marilla and the young lieutenant. From this part of her promise Mary Amber's soul recoiled, for she had no belief that the young leopard with whom she had played at the age of ten could have changed his spots in the course of a few years, or even covered them with a silver bar. But Mary Amber soon saw that her presence at that dinner was an intrinsic part of Miss Marilla's joy in the anticipation of the dinner; and, much as she disliked the position of being flung at the young lieutenant in this way, she promised. After all, what did it matter what he thought of her anyway, since she had no use for him? And then, she could always quietly

freeze him whenever Miss Marilla's
back was turned. And Mary Amber
could freeze with her hazel eyes when
she tried.

So quite early in the morning Miss
Marilla and Mary Amber began a
cheerful stir in Miss Marilla's big sunny
kitchen, and steadily, appetizingly,
there grew an array of salads and pies
and cakes and puddings and cookies and
doughnuts and biscuits and pickles and
olives and jellies; while a great bird
stuffed to bursting went through the
seven stages of its final career to
the oven.

But now it was five o'clock. The
bird with brown and shining breast was
waiting in the oven, "done to a turn;"
mashed potatoes, sweet potatoes, squash,
succotash, and onions had received the
finishing-touches, and had only to be
"taken up." Cranberries and pickles
and celery and jelly gave the final

touches to a perfect table, and the side-
board fairly groaned under its load of
pies and cake. One might have thought
a whole regiment were to dine with
Miss Marilla Chadwick that day, from
the sights and smells that filled the
house. Up in the spare room the fire
glowed in a Franklin heater, and a ge-
ranium glowed in a west window between spotless curtains to welcome the
guest; and now there was nothing left
for the two women to do but the final
anxiety.

Mary Amber had her part in that,
perhaps even more than her hostess and
friend; for Mary Amber was jealous
for Miss Marilla, and Mary Amber
was youthfully incredulous. She had
no trust in Dick Chadwick, even
though he was an officer and had patrol-
led an enemy country for a few months
after the war was over.

Mary Amber had slipped over to her

own house when she finished mashing
the potatoes, and changed her gown.
She was putting little squares of butter on the bread-and-butter plates now,
and the setting sun cast a halo of burnished light over her gold hair, and
brightened up the silk of her brown
gown with its touches of wood-red.
Mary Amber was beautiful to look
upon as she stood with her butterknife
deftly cutting the squares and dropping them in just the right spot on the
plates. But there was a troubled look
in her eyes as she glanced from time
to time at the older woman over by the
window. Miss Marilla had given over
all thought of work, and was intent
only on the road toward the station. It
would seem as if not until this moment
had her great faith failed her, and the
thought come to her that perhaps he
might not come.

"You know, of course, he might not

get that train," she said meditatively.
"The other leaves only half an hour
later. But she said she'd tell him to
take this one."

"That's true, too," said Mary Amber
cheerily. "And nothing will be hurt by
waiting. I've fixed those mashed potatoes so they won't get soggy by being
too hot, and I'm sure they'll keep hot
enough."

"You're a good, dear girl, Mary Amber," said Miss Marilla, giving her a
sudden impulsive kiss. "I only wish I
could do something great and beautiful for you."

Miss Marilla caught up her cape, and
hurried toward the door.

"I'm going out to the gate to meet
him," she said with a smile. "It's time
he was coming in a minute now, and I
want to be out there without hurrying."

She clambered down the steps, her
knees trembling with excitement. She

hoped Mary Amber had not looked out
of the window. A boy was coming
on a bicycle; and, if he should be a boy
with a telegram or a special-delivery
letter, she wanted to read it before
Mary Amber saw her. Oh, how awful
if anything had happened that he
couldn't come to-day! Of course, he
might come later to-night, or to-morrow; and a turkey would keep, though
it was never so good as the minute it
was taken out of the oven.

The boy was almost to the gate now,
and—yes, he was going to stop. He
was swinging one leg out with that
long movement that meant slowing up.
She panted forward with a furtive
glance back at the house. She hoped
Mary Amber was looking at the turkey
and not out of the window.

It seemed that her fingers had suddenly gone tired while she was writing
her name in that boy's book, and they

2

almost refused to tear open the envelope as the boy swung on his wheel again and vanished down the road. She had presence of mind enough to keep her back to the house and the telegram in front of her as she opened it covertly, trying to keep the attitude of still looking eagerly down the road, while the typewritten brief message got itself across to her tumultuous mind.

"Impossible to accept invitation. Have other engagements. Thanks just the same.
"(Signed)
LIEUTENANT RICHARD H. CHADWICK."

Miss Marilla tore the yellow paper hastily, and crumpled it into a ball in her hands as she stared down the road through brimming tears. She managed an upright position; but her knees were shaking under her, and a gone feeling came in her stomach. Across the sunset skies in letters of accusing size there seemed to blaze the paragraphs from *The Springhaven*

Chronicle, copied afterwards in the
county *Gazette,* about Miss Marilla Chadwick's nephew, Lieutenant
Richard H. Chadwick, who was expected at his aunt's home as soon as he
landed in this country after a long
and glorious career in other lands, and
who would spend the week-end with
his aunt, and "doubtless be heard from
at the Springhaven Club House before
he left." Her throat caught with a
queer little sound like a groan. Still,
with her hand grasping the front gate
convulsively, Miss Marilla stood and
stared down the road, trying to think
what to do, how to word a paragraph
explaining why he did not come, how
to explain to Mary Amber so that that
look of sweet incredulousness should
not come into her eyes.

Then suddenly, as she stared
through her blur of tears, there appeared a straggling figure, coming

around the bend of the road by the
Hazard house; and Miss Marilla, with
nothing at all in her mind but to escape
from the watchful, loving eyes of Mary
Amber for a moment longer, till she
could think what to say to her,
staggered out the gate and down the
road toward the person, whoever it was,
that was coming slowly up the road.

On stumbled Miss Marilla, nearer
and nearer to the oncoming man, till
suddenly through a blur of tears she
noticed that he wore a uniform. Her
heart gave a leap, and for a moment she
thought it must be Dick; that he had
been playing her a joke by the telegram, and was coming on immediately
to surprise her before she had a chance
to be disappointed. It was wonderful
how the years had done their halo work
for Dick with Miss Marilla.

She stopped short, trembling, one
hand to her throat. Then, as the man

drew nearer and she saw his halting gait, saw, too, his downcast eyes and whole dejected attitude, she somehow knew it was not Dick. Never would he have walked to her home in that way. There had been a swagger about little Dick that could not be forgotten. The older Dick, crowned now with many honors, would not have forgotten to hold his head high.

Unconscious of her attitude of intense interest she stood with hand still fluttering at her throat, and eyes brightly on the man as he advanced.

When he was almost opposite to her, he looked up. He had fine eyes and good features; but his expression was bitter for one so young, and in the eyes there was a look of pain.

"Oh! excuse me," said Miss Marilla, looking around furtively to be sure Mary Amber could not see them so far away. "Are you in a very great hurry?"

The young man looked surprised, amused, and slightly bored, but paused politely.

"Not specially," he said; and there was a tone of dry sarcasm in his voice. "Is there anything I can do for you?" He lifted the limp little trench-cap, and paused to rest his lame knee.

"Why, I was wondering if you would mind coming in and eating dinner with me," spoke Miss Marilla eagerly from a dry throat of embarrassment. "You see my nephew's a returned soldier, and I've just got word he can't come. The dinner's all ready to be dished up, and it needn't take you long."

"Dinner sounds good to me," said the young man with a grim glimmer of a smile. "I guess I can accommodate you, madam. I haven't had anything to eat since I left the camp last night."

"Oh! You poor child!" said Miss Marilla, beaming on him with a welcoming smile. "Now isn't it fortunate I should have asked *you?*" as if there had been a throng of passing soldiers from which she might have chosen. "But are you sure I'm not keeping you from some one else who is waiting for you?"

"If there's any one else waiting anywhere along this road for me, it's all news to me, madam; and anyhow you got here first, and I guess you have first rights."

He had swung into the easy, familiar vernacular of the soldier now; and for the moment his bitterness was held in abeyance, and the really nice look in his eyes shone forth.

"Well, then, we'll just go along in," said Miss Marilla, casting another quick glance toward the house. "And I think I'm most fortunate to have found you. It's so disappointing to

get dinner ready for company and then
not have any."

"Must be almost as disappointing as
to get all ready for dinner and then not
have any," said the soldier affably.

Miss Marilla smiled wistfully.

"I suppose your name doesn't happen to be Richard, does it?" she asked
with that childish appeal in her eyes
that had always kept her a young
woman and good company for Mary
Amber, even though her hair had long
been gray.

"Might just as well be that as anything else," he responded, affably, willing to drop into whatever rôle was set
for him in this most unexpected byplay.

"And you wouldn't mind if I should
call you Dick?" she asked with a wistful
look in her blue eyes.

"Like nothing better," he assented
glibly, and found his own heart warm-
ing to this confiding stranger lady.

"That's beautiful of you!" She put out a shy hand, and laid it lightly on the edge of his cuff. "You don't know how much obliged I am. You see, Mary Amber hasn't ever quite believed he was coming — Dick, I mean — and she's been so kind, and helped me get the dinner and all. I just couldn't bear to tell her he wasn't coming."

The young soldier stopped short in the middle of the road, and whistled.

"Horrors!" he exclaimed in dismay "Are there other guests? Who is Mary Amber?"

"Why, she's just my neighbor, who played with you—I mean with Dick when he was here visiting as a child a good many years ago. I'm afraid he wasn't always as polite to her then as a boy ought to be to a little girl; and— well, she's never liked him very well. I was afraid she would say, 'I told you so' if she thought he didn't come. It won't be necessary for me to tell any lies, you know. I'll just say, 'Dick, this is Mary Amber; I suppose you don't remember her,' and that'll be all. You don't mind, do you? It won't take long to eat dinner."

"But I'm a terrible mess to meet a girl!" he exclaimed uneasily, looking down deprecatingly at himself. "I thought it was just you. This uniform's three sizes too large, and needs a drink. Besides," he passed a speculative hand over his smoothly shaven chin, "I—don't *care* for girls!" There was a deep frown between his eyes, and the bitter look had come back on his face. Miss Marilla thought he looked as if he might be going to run away.

"Oh, that's all right!" said Miss Marilla anxiously. "Neither does Mary Amber like men. She says they're all a selfish conceited lot. You needn't have much to do with her. Just eat your dinner and tell anything you want to about the war. We won't bother you to talk much. Come; this is the house, and the turkey must be on the table getting cold by now."

She swung open the gate, and laid a persuasive hand on the shabby sleeve; and the young man reluctantly followed her up the path to the front door.

CHAPTER II

When Lyman Gage set sail for France three years before, he left behind him a modest interest in a promising business enterprise, a girl who seemed to love him dearly, and a debt of several thousand dollars to her father, who had advised him to go into the enterprise and furnished the funds for his share in the capital.

When he had returned from France three days before, he had been met with news that the business enterprise had gone to smash during the war, the girl had become engaged to a dashing young captain with a well-feathered nest, and the debt had become a galling yoke.

"Father says, tell you you need not worry about the money you owe him," wrote the girl sweetly, concluding her revelations. "You can pay it at your leisure when you get started again."

Lyman Gage lost no time in gathering together every cent he could scrape up. This was more than he had at first hoped, because of the fact that he owned two houses in the big city in which he had landed; and these houses, though old and small, happened to be located in the vicinity of a great industrial plant that had sprung up since the end of the war, and houses were going at soaring prices. They were snapped up at once at a sum that was fabulous in comparison with their real value. This, with what he had brought home and the bonus he received on landing, exactly covered his indebtedness to the man who was to have been his father-in-law; and, when he turned away from the window where he had been telegraphing the money to his lawyer in a far State with instructions to pay the loan at once, he had just forty-six cents left in his pocket.

Suddenly, as he reflected that he had done the last thing there was left that he now cared to do on earth, the noises of the great city got hold upon his nerve, and tore and racked it.

He was filled with a great desire to get out and away from it, he cared not where, only so that the piercing sounds and rumbling grind of the traffic of the city should not press upon the raw nerves and torture them.

With no thought of getting anything to eat or providing for a shelterless night that was fast coming on, he wandered out into the train-area of the great station, and idly read the names up over the train-gates. One caught his fancy, "PURLING BROOK." It seemed as if it might be quiet there, and a fellow could think. He followed the impulse, and strode through the gates just as they were about to be closed. Dropping into the last seat in the car as the train was about to start, he flung his head back, and closed his eyes wearily. He did not care whether he ever got anywhere or not. He was weary in heart and spirit. He wished that he might just sink away into noth ingness. He was too tired to think, to bemoan his fate, to touch with torturing finger of memory all the little beautiful hopes that he had woven about the girl he thought he loved better than any one else on earth. Just passingly he had a wish that he had a living mother to whom he could go with his sick heart for healing. But she had been gone long years, and his father even longer. There was really no one to whom he cared to show his face, now that all he had counted dear on earth had been suddenly taken from him.

The conductor roused him from a

profound sleep, demanding a ticket, and he had the good fortune to remember the name he had seen over the gate: "Purling Brook. How much?"

"Fifty-six cents."

Gage reached into his pocket, and displayed the coins on his palm with a wry smile.

"Guess you better put me off here, and I'll walk," he said, stumbling wearily to his feet.

"That's all right, son. Sit down," said the conductor half roughly. "You pay me when you come back sometime. I'll make it good." And he glanced at the uniform kindly.

Gage looked down at his shabby self helplessly. Yes, he was still a soldier, and people had not got over the habit of being kind to the uniform. He thanked the conductor, and sank into sleep again, to be roused by the same kindly hand a few minutes later at Purling Brook. He stumbled off, and stood looking dazedly about him at the trig little village. The sleep was not yet gone from his eyes, nor the ache from his nerves; but the clear quiet of the little town seemed to wrap him about soothingly like salve, and the crisp air entered into his lungs, and gave him heart. He realized that he was hungry.

It seemed to have been a popular afternoon train that he had travelled upon. He looked beyond the groups of happy home-comers to where it hurried away gustily down the track, even then preparing to stop at the next near suburban station to deposit a few more home-comers. There on that train went the only friend he felt he had in the world at present, that grizzly conductor with his kindly eyes looking through great bifocals like a pleasant old grasshopper.

3

Well, he could not remain here any longer. The air was biting, and the sun was going down. Across the road the little drug-store even then was twinkling out with lights behind its blue and green glass urns. Two boys and a girl were drinking something at the soda-fountain through straws, and laughing a great deal. It somehow turned him sick, he could not tell why. He had done things like that many a time himself.

There was a little stone church down the street, with a spire and bells. The sun touched the bells with burnished crimson till they looked like Christmas cards. A youthful rural football team went noisily across the road, discoursing about how they would come out that night if their mothers would let them; and the station cab came down the street full of passengers, and waited for a lady at the meat-market. He could see the legs of a chicken sticking out of the basket as the driver helped her in.

He began to wonder why he hadn't stayed in the city and spent his forty-six cents for something to eat. It would have bought a great many crackers, say, or even bananas. He passed the bakery, and a whiff of fresh-baked bread greeted his nostrils. He cast a wistful eye at the window. Of course he might go in and ask for a job in payment for his supper. There were his soldier's clothes. But no. That was equivalent to begging. He could not quite do that. Here in town they would have all the help they wanted. Perhaps, farther out in the country—perhaps—he didn't know what; only he couldn't bring himself to ask for food, even with the offer to work. He didn't care enough for that. What was hunger, anyway? A thing to be satisfied and come again. What

would happen if he didn't satisfy it?
Die, of course, but what did it matter?
What was there to live for, anyway?

He passed a house all windows,
where children were gathered about a
piano with one clumsily playing an ac-
companiment. There was an open fire,
and the long windows came down to the
piazza floor. They were singing at the
top of their lungs, the old, time-worn
song made familiar to them by com-
munity sing-songs, still good to them
because they all knew it so well,

> "There's a long, long trail a-winding
> Until my dreams all come true;"

and it gripped his heart like a knife. He
had sung that song with *her* when it was
new and tender, just before he sailed
away; and the trail had seemed so long!
And now he had reached the end of it,
and she had not been there to meet him!
It was incredible! She so fair! And
false! After all those months of wait-

ing! That was the hardest part of it, that she could have done it, and then explained so lightly that he had been away so long she was sure he would understand, and they both must have got over their childish attachment; and so on, through the long, nauseating sentences of her repeal. He shuddered as he said them over to his tired heart, and then shuddered again with the keen air; for his uniform was thin, and he had no overcoat.

What was that she had said about the money? He needn't worry about it. A sort of bone to toss to the lone dog after he was kicked out. Ah, well! It was paid. He was glad of that. He was even grimly glad for his own destitution. It gave a kind of sense of satisfaction to have gone hungry and homeless to pay it all in one grand lump, and to have paid it at once, and through his lawyer, without any word to her or her

father either. They should not be even
distant witnesses of his humiliation.
He would never cross their path again
if he had his way. They should be as
completely wiped out of his existence
and he out of theirs as if the same universe did not hold them.

He passed down the broad, pleasant
street in the crisp air, and every home
on either hand gave him a thrust of
memory that stabbed him to the heart.
It was such a home as one of these that
he had hoped to have some day, although it would have been in the city,
perhaps, for she always liked the city.
He had hoped in the depths of his heart
to persuade her to the country, though.
Now he saw as in a revelation how futile
such hopes had been. She would never
have come to love sweet, quiet ways
such as he loved. She couldn't ever
have really loved him, or she would have
waited, would not have changed.

Over and over again he turned the bitter story, trying to get it settled in his heart so that the sharp edges would not hurt so, trying to accustom himself to the thought that she whom he had cherished through the blackness of the years that were past was not what he had thought her. He stopped in the road beside a tall hedge that hid the Hazard house from view, and snatched out her picture that he had carried in his breast pocket till now; snatched it out, gazed upon it with a look that was not good to see on a young face, and tore it across! He took a step forward, and every step he tore a tiny fragment from the picture and flung it into the road bit by bit till the lovely face was mutilated in the dust where the feet of passers-by would grind upon it and where those great blue eyes that had gazed back at him from the picture so long would be destroyed forever. It was the last thread that bound him to her, that picture; and, when the last scrap of picture had fluttered away from him, he put his head down and strode forward like one who has cast away from him his last hope.

The voice of Miss Marilla roused him like a homely, pleasant sound about the house of a morning when one has had an unhappy dream; and he lifted his head, and, soldier-like, dropped into the old habit of hiding his emotions.

Her kindly face somehow comforted him, and the thought of dinner was a welcome one. The ugly tragedy of his life seemed to melt away for the moment, as if it could not stand the light of the setting sun and her wholesome presence. There was an appeal in her eyes that reached him; and somehow he didn't feel like turning down her naïve, childlike proposition. Besides, he was used to being cared for because he was

a soldier, and why not once more now
when everything else had gone so rot-
ten? It was an adventure, anyway,
and what was there left for him but adventure? he asked himself with a little
bitter sneer.

But, when she mentioned a *girl*, that
was a different thing! Girls were all
treacherous. It was a new conviction
with him; but it had gone deep, so deep
that it had extended not only to a certain girl or class of girls, but to all girls
everywhere. He had become a woman-
hater. He wanted nothing more to do
with any of them. And yet at that
moment his tired, disappointed, hurt
man's soul was really crying out for
the woman of the universe to comfort
him, to explain to him this awful cir-
cumstance that had come to all his
bright dreams. A mother, that was
what he thought he wanted; and Miss
Marilla looked as if she might make

a nice mother. So he turned like a tired little hungry boy, and followed her, at least until she said "girl." Then he almost turned and fled.

Yet, while Miss Marilla coaxed and explained about Mary Amber, he stood facing again the lovely vision of the girl he had left behind at the beginning of the long, long trail, and whose picture he had just trampled underfoot on this end of the trail, which it now seemed to him would wind on forever alone for him. As he paused on Miss Marilla's immaculate front steps, he was preparing himself to face the enemy of his life in the form of woman. The one thing really that made him go into that house and meekly submit to be Miss Marilla's guest was that his soul had risen to battle. He would fight Girl in the concrete! She should be his enemy from henceforth. And this strange, unknown girl, who hated men and thought

them conceited and selfish, this cold, in-
human creature, was likely false-
hearted too, like the one he had loved
and who had not loved him. He would
show her what he thought of such girls,
of all girls; what all men who knew anything about it thought of all girls! And,
thus reasoning, he followed Miss Marilla into the pleasant oilcloth-covered
hall, and up the front stairs to the spare
room, where she smilingly showed him
the towels and brushes prepared for his
comfort, and left him, calling cheerily
back that dinner would be on the table
as soon as he was ready to come down.

All the time he was bathing his tired,
dirty face and cold, rough hands in the
warm, sweet-scented soap-suds, and
wiping them on the fragrant towel,
even while he stood in front of the mir-
ror all polished to reflect the visage of
Lieutenant Richard H. Chadwick, and
brushed his close-cropped curls till

there was not a hint of wave left in
them, he was hardening himself to meet
Girl in the concrete and get back a return for what she had done to his life.

Then, with a last final polish of the
brush and a flick of the whisk-broom
over his discouraged-looking uniform,
he set his lips grimly, and went down-
stairs, taking the precaution to fold his
cap and put it into his pocket, for he
might want to escape at any minute,
and it was best to be prepared.

CHAPTER III

Mary Amber was bearing in the great platter of golden-brown turkey when he first saw her, and had not heard him come down. She was entirely off her guard, with a sweet, serious intentness upon her work and a stray wisp of gold hair set afloat across the kitchen-flushed cheek. She looked so sweet and serviceable and true, with her lips parted in the pleasure of the final completion of her task, that the soldier was taken by surprise and thrown entirely off his guard. Was this the false-hearted creature he had come to fight?

Then Mary Amber felt his eyes upon her as he stood staring from the open hall door, and, lifting her own clear ones, froze into the opponent at once. A very polite opponent, it is true, with all the grace of a young queen, but nevertheless an opponent, cold as a young icicle.

Miss Marilla with bright eyes and preternaturally pink cheeks spoke into the vast pause that suddenly surrounded them all, and her voice sounded strangely unnatural to herself.

"Dick, this is Mary Amber; I suppose you don't remember her."

And the young soldier, not yet quite recovered from that first sweet vision of Mary Amber, went forward with his belligerence to woman somewhat held in abeyance.

"You—have changed a good deal since then, haven't you?" he managed to ask with his native quickness to say the right thing in an emergency.

"A good many years have passed," she said, coolly putting out a reluctant hand to please Miss Marilla. "You

don't look at all as you did. I never
should have known you."

The girl was looking keenly at him,
studying his face closely. If a soldier
just home from an ocean trip could get
any redder, his face would have grown
so under her scrutiny. Also, now he
was face to face with her, he felt his
objection to Girl in general receding
before the fact of his own position.
How had that ridiculous old woman expected him to carry off a situation like
this without giving it away? How was
he supposed to converse with a girl he
had never seen before, about things he
had never done,—with a girl with whom
he was supposed to have played in his
youth? Why had he been such a fool
as to get into this corner just for the
sake of one more dinner? Why, to-
morrow he would need another dinner,
and all the to-morrows through which
he might have to live. What was one

dinner more or less? He felt in his hip pocket for the comforting assurance of his cap, and gave a furtive glance toward the hall door. It wouldn't be far to bolt back to the road, and what would be the difference? He would never see either of the two again.

Then the sweet, anxious eyes of his hostess met his with an appealing smile and he felt himself powerless to move.

The girl's eyes had swept over his ill-fitting uniform and he seemed to feel every crease and stain.

"I thought they told us you were an officer, but I don't see your bars." She laughed mockingly, and searched his face again accusingly.

"This is another fellow's uniform," he answered lamely. "Mine got shrunk so I could hardly get into it, and another fellow who was going home changed with me."

He lifted his eyes frankly, for it was

the truth that he told, and he looked into her eyes, but saw that she did not believe him. Her dislike and distrust of the little boy Dick had come to the front. He saw that she believed that Dick had been boasting to his aunt of honors that were not his. A wave of anger swept over his face; yet somehow he could not summon his defiance. Somehow he wanted her to believe him.

They sat down at the beautiful table, and the turkey got in its work on his poor human sensibilities. The delicate perfume of the hot meat as it fell in large, flaky slices from Miss Marilla's sharp knife, the whiff of the summer savory and sage and sweet marjoram in the stuffing, the smoothness of the mashed potatoes, the brownness of the candied sweet potatoes, all cried out to him and held him prisoner. The odor of the food brought a giddiness to his head, and the faintness of hunger at-

tacked him. A pallor grew under the
tan of his face, and there were dark
shadows under his nice eyes that quite
touched Miss Marilla, and almost softened the hard look of distrust that had
been growing around Mary Amber's
gentle lips.

"This certainly is great!" he murmured. "I don't deserve to get in on
anything like this, but I'm no end
grateful."

Mary Amber's questioning eyes re-
called him in confusion to his rôle of
nephew in the house, and he was glad of
the chance to bend his head while Miss
Marilla softly asked a blessing on the
meal. He had been wont to think he
could get away with any situation; but
he began to feel now as if his recent
troubles had unnerved him, and he
might make a mess of this one. Somehow that girl seemed as if she could see
into a fellow's heart. Why couldn't he

show her how he despised the whole race
of false-hearted womankind?

They heaped his plate with good
things, poured him amber coffee rich
with cream, gave him cranberry sauce
and pickles and olives, and passed little
delicate biscuits, and butter with the
fragrance of roses. With all this before him he suddenly felt as if he could
not swallow a mouthful. He lifted his
eyes to the opposite wall, and a neatly
framed sentence in quaint old English
lettering met his eye, "Who crowneth
thee with loving-kindness and tender
mercies, so that thy youth is renewed
like the eagle's."

An intense desire to put his head
down on the table and cry came over
him. The warmth of the room, the
fragrance of the food, had made him
conscious of an ache in every part of
his body. His head was throbbing too,
and he wondered what was the matter

with him. After all the harshness of the world, and the bitterness, to meet a kindness like this seemed to unnerve him. But gradually the food got in its work, and the hot coffee stimulated him. He rose to the occasion greatly. He described France, spoke of the beautiful cathedrals he had seen, the works of art, the little children, the work of reconstruction that was going on, spoke of Germany too, when he saw they expected him to have been there, although this was a shoal on which he almost wrecked his rôle before he realized. He told of the voyage over and the people he had met, and he kept most distinctly away from anything personal, at least as far away as Mary Amber would let him. She with her keen, questioning eyes was always bringing up some question that was almost impossible for him to answer directly without treading on dangerous ground, and it required skill indeed to turn her from it. Mary listened and marvelled, trying continually to trace in his face the lines of the fat-faced, arrogant child who used to torment her.

Mary rose to take the plates, and the young soldier insisted on helping. Miss Marilla, pleased to see them getting on so nicely, sat smiling in her place, reaching out to brush away a stray crumb on the table-cloth. Mary, lingering in the kitchen for a moment, to be sure the fire was not being neglected, lifted the stove-lid, and with the draught a little flame leaped up around a crumpled, smoldering yellow paper with the familiar "Western Union Telegraph" heading. Three words stood out distinctly for a second, "Impossible to accept," and then were enveloped by the flame. Mary stood and stared with the stove-lid in her hand, and then, as the flame curled the paper

over, she saw "Lieutenant Richard—"
revealed and immediately licked up by
the flame.

It lay, a little crisp, black fabric
with its message utterly illegible, but
still Mary stood and stared and wondered. She had seen the boy on the
bicycle ride up and go away. She had
also seen the approaching soldier almost immediately, and the thought of
the telegram had been at once erased.
Now it came back forcefully. Dick,
then, had sent a telegram, and it looked
as if he had declined the invitation.
Who, then, was this stranger at the
table? Some comrade working Miss
Marilla for a dinner, or Dick himself,
having changed his mind or playing a
practical joke? In any case Mary felt
she ought to disapprove of him utterly.
It was her duty to show him up to Miss
Marilla; and yet how could she do it

when she did not know anything
herself?

"Hurry, Mary, and bring the pie,"
called Miss Marilla. "We're waiting."

Mary put the stove-lid down, and
went slowly, thoughtfully back to the
dining-room bearing a pie. She studied
the face of the young soldier intently
as she passed him his pie, but he seemed
so young and pleasant and happy she
hadn't the heart to say anything just
yet. She would bide her time. Perhaps somehow it was all explainable.
So she set to asking him questions.

"By the way, Dick, what ever be-
came of Barker?" she requested, fixing
her clear eyes on his face.

"Barker?" said Lyman Gage, puz-
zled and polite, then, remembering his
rôle, "Oh, yes, *Barker!*" He laughed.
"Great old Barker, wasn't he?" He
turned in troubled appeal to Miss
Marilla.

"Barker certainly was the cutest little guinea-pig I ever saw," beamed Miss Marilla, "although at the time I really wasn't as fond of it as you were. You would have it around in the kitchen so much."

There was covert apology in Miss Marilla's voice for the youthful character of the young man he was supposed to be.

"I should judge I must have been a good deal of a nuisance in those days," hazarded the soldier, feeling that he was treading on dangerous ground.

"Oh, no!" sighed Miss Marilla, trying to be truthful and at the same time polite. "Children will be children, you know."

"All children are not alike." It was as near to snapping as sweet Mary Amber ever came. She had memories which time had not dimmed.

"Was it as bad as that?" laughed the young man. "I'm sorry!"

Mary had to laugh. His frankness certainly was disarming. But there was that telegram! And Mary grew serious again. She did not intend to have her gentle old friend deceived.

Mary insisted on clearing off the table and washing the dishes, and the soldier insisted on helping her; so Miss Marilla, much disturbed that domestic duties should interfere with the evening, put everything away, and made the task as brief as possible, looking anxiously at Mary Amber every trip back from the refrigerator and pantry to see how she was getting on with the strange soldier, and how the strange soldier was getting on with her. At first she was a little troubled lest he shouldn't be the kind of man she would want to introduce to Mary Amber; but after she had heard him talk and ex-

press such thoroughly wholesome
views on politics and national subjects
she almost forgot he was not the real
Dick, and her doting heart could not
help wanting Mary Amber to like him.
He was, in fact, the personification of
the Dick she had dreamed out for her
own, as different in fact from the real
Dick as could have been imagined, and
a great deal better. His frank eyes, his
pleasant manner, his cultured voice, all
pleased her; and she couldn't help feeling that he was Dick come back as she
would have liked him to be all the time.

"I'd like to have a little music, just
a little before Mary has to go home,"
Miss Marilla said wistfully as Mary
Amber hung up the dish-towel with an
air that said plainly without words that
she felt her duty toward the stranger
was over and she was going to depart
at once.

"Sure!" said the stranger. "You sing, don't you, Miss Mary?"

There was nothing for it, and Mary resigned herself to another half hour. They went into the parlor; and Mary sat down at the old square piano, and touched its asthmatic keys that sounded the least bit tin-panny even under such skilled fingers as hers.

"What shall I play?" questioned Mary. " 'The long, long trail'?" There was a bit of sarcasm in her tone. Mary was a real musician, and hated rag-time.

"No! *Never!*" said the soldier quickly. "I mean—not that, *please;*" and a look of such bitter pain swept over his face that Mary glanced up surprised, and forgot to be disagreeable for several minutes while she pondered his expression.

"Excuse me," he said. "But I loathe it. Give us something else; sing some-

thing *real*. I'm sure you can." There
was a hidden compliment in his tone,
and Mary was surprised. The soldier
had almost forgotten that he did not be-
long there. He was acting as he might
have acted in his own social sphere.

Mary struck a few chords tenderly
on the piano, and then broke into the
delicious melody of "The Spirit
Flower;" and Lyman Gage forgot that
he was playing a part in a strange
home with a strange girl, forgot that he
hadn't a cent in the world, and his girl
was gone, and sat watching her face
as she sang. For Mary had a voice
like a thrush in the summer evening,
that liquid appeal that always reminds
one of a silver spoon dropped into a
glass of water; and Mary had a face
like the spirit flower itself. As she
sang she could not help living, breathing, being the words she spoke.

There was nothing, absolutely noth-

ing, about Mary to remind him of the
girl he had lost; and there was something in her sweet, serious demeanor as
she sang to call to his better nature; a
wholesome, serious sweetness that was
in itself a kind of antiseptic against bitterness and sweeping denunciation.
Lyman Gage as he listened was lifted
out of himself and set in a new world
where men and women thought of
something besides money and position
and social prestige. He seemed to be
standing off apart from himself and
seeing himself from a new angle, an
angle in which he was not the only one
that mattered in this world, and in
which he got a hint that his plans might
be only hindrances to a larger life for
himself and every one else. Not that he
exactly thought these things in so many
words. It was more as if while Mary
sang a wind blew freshly from a place
where such thoughts were crowding,

and made him seem smaller in his own conceit than he had thought he was.

"And now sing 'Laddie,'" pleaded Miss Marilla.

A wave of annoyance swept over Mary Amber's face. It was plain she did not wish to sing that song. Nevertheless, she sang it, forgetting herself and throwing all the pathos and tenderness into her voice that belonged to the beautiful words. Then she turned from the piano decidedly, and rose. "I must go home at once," was written in every line of her attitude. Miss Marilla rose nervously, and looked from one of her guests to the other.

"Dick, I wonder if you haven't learned to sing."

Her eyes were so pathetic that they stirred the young man to her service. Besides, there was something so contemptuous in the attitude of that human spirit flower standing on the wing

as it were in that done-with-him-for-
ever attitude that spurred him into a
faint desire to show her what he
could do.

"Why, sure!" he answered lazily, and
with a stride transferred himself to the
piano-stool and struck a deep, strong
chord or two. Suddenly there poured
forth a wondrous barytone such as was
seldom heard in Purling Brook, and
indeed is not common anywhere. He
had a feeling that he was paying for his
wonderful dinner, and must do his best.
The first song that had come to his
mind was a big, blustery French patri-
otic song; and the very spirit of the
march was in its cadence. Out of the
corner of his eye he could see Mary
Amber still poised, but waiting in her
astonishment. He felt that he had already scored a point. When he came
to the grand climax, she cried out with
pleasure and clapped her hands. Miss

Marilla had sunk into the mahogany rocker, but was sitting on the edge, alert to prolong this gala evening; and two bright spots of colorful delight shone on her faded cheeks.

He did not wait for them to ask him for another; he dashed into a minor key, and began to sing a wild, sweet, sobbing song of love and loss till Mary, entranced, softly slipped into a chair, and sat breathless with clasped hands and shining eyes. It was such an artistic, perfect thing, that song, that she forgot everything else while it was going on.

When the last sob died away, and the little parlor was silent with deep feeling, he whirled about on the piano-stool, and rose briskly.

"Now I've done my part, am I to be allowed to see the lady home?"

He looked at Miss Marilla instead of

Mary for permission, and she smiled, half frightened.

"It isn't necessary at all," spoke Mary crisply, rising and going for a wrap. "It's only a step."

"Oh, I think so, surely!" answered Miss Marilla as if a great point of etiquette had been decided. She gave him a look of perfect trust.

"It's only across the garden and through the hedge, you know," she said in a low tone; "but I think she would appreciate it."

"Certainly," he said, and turned with perfect courtesy as Mary looked in at the door and called, "Good night."

He did not make a fuss about attending her. He simply was there close beside her as she sped through the dark without a word to him.

"It's been very pleasant to meet you," he said as she turned with a motion of dismissal at her own steps, "again," he

5

added lamely. "I—I've enjoyed the evening more than you can understand. I enjoyed your singing."

"Oh! *My* singing!" flung back Mary. "Why, I was like a sparrow beside a nightingale. It wasn't quite fair of you to let me sing first without knowing you had a voice. It's strange. You know you never used to sing."

It seemed to him her glance went deep as she looked at him through the shadows of the garden. He thought about it as he crept back through the hedge, shivering now, for the night was keen and his uniform was thin. Well, what did it matter what she thought? He would soon be far away from her and never likely to see her again. Yet he was glad he had scored a point, one point against Girl in the concrete.

Now he must go in and bid his hostess good-by, and then away to—where?

CHAPTER IV

As Lyman Gage went up the steps to Miss Marilla's front porch a sick thrill of cold and weariness passed over his big frame. Every joint and muscle seemed to cry out in protest, and his very vitals seemed sore and racked. The bit of bright evening was over, and he was facing his own gray life again with a future that was void and empty.

But the door was not shut. Miss Marilla was hovering anxiously inside with the air of just having retreated from the porch. She gave a little relieved gasp as he entered.

"Oh, I was afraid you wouldn't come back," she said eagerly. "And I did so want to thank you and tell you how we—how I—yes, I mean *we,* for I know she loved that singing—how very much we have enjoyed it. I shall always thank God that He sent you along just then."

"Well, I certainly have cause to thank you for that wonderful dinner," he said earnestly, as he might have spoken to a dear relation, "and for all this"—he waved his big hand toward the bright room—"this pleasantness. It was like coming home, and I haven't any home to come to now."

"Oh! Haven't you?" said Miss Marilla caressingly." "Oh, *haven't* you?" she said again wistfully. "I wonder why I can't keep you a little while, then. You seem just like my own nephew— as I had hoped he would be—I haven't seen him in a long time. Where were you going when I stopped you?"

The young man lifted heavy eyes that were bloodshot and sore to the turning, and tried to smile. To save his life he couldn't lie blithely when it seemed so good to be in that warm room.

"Why—I was—I don't know—I guess I just wasn't going anywhere. To tell you the truth, I was all in, and down on my luck, and as blue as indigo when you met me. I was just tramping anywhere to get away from it."

"You poor boy!" said Miss Marilla, putting out her fine little blue-veined hands and caressing the old khaki sleeve. "Well, then you're just going to stay with me and get rested. There's no reason in the world why you shouldn't."

"No, indeed!" said Lyman Gage, drawing himself up bravely, "I couldn't think of it. It wouldn't be right. But I certainly thank you with all my heart for what you have done for me to-night. I really must go at once."

"But where?" she asked pathetically, as if he belonged to her, sliding her hands detainingly down to his big rough ones.

"Oh, anywhere, it doesn't matter!" he said, holding her delicate little old hand in his with a look of sacred respect as if a nice old angel had offered to hold hands with him. "I'm a soldier, you know; and a few storms more or less won't matter. I'm used to it. Good night."

He clasped her hands a moment, and was about to turn away; but she held his fingers eagerly.

"You shall not go that way!" she declared. "Out into the cold without any overcoat, and no home to go to! Your hands are hot, too. I believe you have a fever. You're going to stay here to-night and have a good sleep and a warm breakfast; and then, if you must go, all right. My spare bed is all made up, and there's a fire in the Franklin heater. The room's as warm

as toast, and Mary put a big bouquet
of chrysanthemums up there. If you
don't sleep there, it will all be wasted.
You *must* stay."

"No, it wouldn't be right." He
shook his head again, and smiled wistfully. "What would people say?"

"Say! Why, they've got it in the
paper that you're to be here—at least,
that Dick's to be here. They'll think
you're my nephew and think nothing
else about it. Besides, I guess I have
a right to have company if I like."

"If there was any way I could pay
you," said the young man. "But I
haven't a cent to my name, and no telling how long before I will have anything. I really couldn't accept any
such hospitality."

"Oh, that's all right," said Miss Marilla cheerily. "You can pay me if you
like, sometime when you get plenty; or
perhaps you'll take me in when I'm

having a hard time. Anyhow, you're going to stay. I won't take no for an answer. I've been disappointed and disappointed about Dick's coming, and me having no one to show for all the years of the war, just making sweaters for the world, it seemed like, with no one belonging to me; and now I've got a soldier, and I'm going to keep him at least for one night. Nobody's to know but you're my own nephew, and I haven't got to go around the town, have I, telling that Dick didn't care enough for his old country aunt to come out and take dinner with her? It's nothing to them, is it, if they think he came and stayed overnight too? Or even a few days. Nobody 'll be any the wiser, and I'll take a lot more comfort."

"I'd like to accommodate you," faltered the soldier; "but you know I really ought—" Suddenly the big fellow was seized with a fit of sneezing, and the sick sore thrills danced all down his back, and slapped him in the face, and pricked him in the throat, and banged against his head. He dropped weakly down in a chair, and got out the discouragedest-looking handkerchief that ever a soldier carried. It looked as if it might have washed the decks on the way over, or wiped off shoes, as doubtless it had; and it left a dull streak of olive-drab dust on his cheek and chin when he had finished polishing off the last sneeze and lifted his suffering eyes to his hostess.

"You're sick!" declared Miss Marilla with a kind of satisfaction, as if now she had got something she could really take hold of. "I've thought it all the evening. I first laid it to the wind in your face, for I knew you weren't the drinking kind; and then I thought maybe you'd had to be up all night last night or something; lack of sleep makes eyes look that way; but I believe you've got the grippe, and I'm going to put you to bed and give you some homeopathic medicine. Come, tell me the truth. Aren't you chilly?"

With a half-sheepish smile the soldier admitted that he was, and a big involuntary shudder ran over his tall frame with the admission.

"Well, it's high time we got to work. There's plenty of hot water; and you go up to the bathroom, and take a hot bath. I'll put a hot-water bag in the bed, and get it good and warm; and I've got a long, warm flannel nightgown I guess you can get on. It was made for grandmother, and she was a big woman. Come, we'll go right upstairs. I can come down and shut up the house while you're taking your bath."

The soldier protested, but Miss Marilla swept all before her. She locked the front door resolutely, and put the chain on. She turned out the parlor light, and shoved the young man before her to the stairs.

"But I oughtn't to," he protested again with one foot on the first step. "I'm an utter stranger."

"Well, what's that?" said Miss Marilla crisply. " 'I was a stranger, and ye took me in.' When it comes to that, we're all strangers. Come, hurry up; you ought to be in bed. You'll feel like a new man when I get you tucked up."

"You're awfully good," he murmured, stumbling up the stairs, with a sick realization that he was giving way to the little imps of chills and thrills that were dancing over him, that he was all in, and in a few minutes more he would be a contemptible coward, letting a lone, old woman fuss over him this way.

Miss Marilla turned up the light,

and threw back the covers of the spare bed, sending a whiff of lavender through the room. The Franklin heater glowed cheerfully, and the place was warm as toast. There was something sweet and homelike in the old-fashioned room with its queer, ancient framed photographs of people long gone, and its plain but fine old mahogany. The soldier raised his bloodshot eyes, and looked about with a thankful wish that he felt well enough to appreciate it all.

Miss Marilla had pulled open a drawer, and produced a long, fine flannel garment of nondescript fashion; and from a closet she drew forth a long pink bathrobe and a pair of felt slippers.

"There! I guess you can get those on."

She bustled into the bathroom, turned on the hot water, and heaped big white bath-towels and sweet-scented soap upon him. In a kind of daze of thankfulness he stumbled into the bath-room, and began his bath. He hadn't had a bath like that in—was it two years? Somehow the hot water held down the nasty little sick thrills, and cut out the chills for the time. It was wonderful to feel clean and warm, and smell the freshness of the towels and soap. He climbed into the big night-gown which also smelled of lavender, and came forth presently with the felt slippers on the front of his feet, and the pink bathrobe trailing around his shoulders. There was a meek, con-quered expression on his face; and he crept gratefully into the warm bed ac-cording to directions, and snuggled down with that sick, sore thrill of thankfulness that everybody who has ever had grippe knows.

Miss Marilla bustled up from downstairs with a second hot-water bag in one hand and a thermometer in the other.

"I'm going to take your temperature," she said briskly, and stuck the thermometer into his unresisting mouth. Somehow it was wonderfully sweet to be fussed over this way, almost like having a mother. He hadn't had such care since he was a little fellow in the hospital at prep school.

"I thought so!" said Miss Marilla, casting a practised eye at the thermometer a moment later. "You've got quite a fever; and you've got to lie right still, and do as I say, or you'll have a time of it. I hate to think what would have happened to you if I'd been weak enough to let you go off into the cold without any overcoat to-night."

"Oh, I'd have walked it off likely," faintly spoke the old Adam in the sleepy, sick soldier; but he knew as he spoke that he was lying, and he knew Miss Marilla knew it also. He would have laughed if it hadn't been too much trouble. It was wonderful to be in a bed like this, and be warm, and that ache in his back against the hot-water bag! It almost made his head stop aching.

In almost no time at all he was asleep. He never realized when Miss Marilla brought a glass, and fed him medicine. He opened his mouth obediently when she told him, and went right on sleeping.

"Bless his heart!" she said. "He must have been all worn out;" and she turned the light low, and gathering up his chairful of clothes, slipped away to the bathroom, where presently they were all, except the shoes, soaking in strong, hot soap-suds, and Miss Marilla had gone downstairs to stir up the fire and put on irons. But she took the precaution to close all the blinds on the

Amber side of the house, and pull down
the shades. Mary had no need ever to
find out what she was doing.

The night wore on, and Miss Marilla
wrought with happy heart and willing
hands. She was doing something for
somebody who really needed it, and who
for the time being had no one else to do
for him. He was hers exclusively to be
served this night. It was years since
she had had anybody of her own to care
for, and she luxuriated in the service.

Every hour she slipped up to feel
his forehead, listen to his breathing,
and give him his medicine, and then
slipped down to the kitchen again to her
ironing. Garment by garment the soldier's meagre outfit came from the
steaming suds, was conveyed to the
kitchen, where it hung on an improvised
line over the range, and got itself dry
enough to be ironed and patched. It
was a work of love, and therefore it

was done perfectly. When morning dawned the soldier's outfit, thoroughly renovated and pressed almost beyond recognition, lay on a chair by the spare-room window, and Miss Marilla in her dark-blue serge morning-dress lay tidily down on the outside of her bed to take "forty winks." But even then she could hardly get to sleep, she was so excited thinking about her guest and wondering whether he would feel better when he awoke or whether she ought to send for a doctor.

A hoarse cough roused her an hour later, and she went with speed to her patient, and found him tossing and battling in his sleep with some imaginary foe.

"I don't owe you a cent any longer!" he declared fiercely. "I've paid it all, even to the interest while I was in France; and there's no reason why I shouldn't tell you just what I think of

6

you. You can go to thunder with your kind offers. I'm off *you* for life!" And then the big fellow turned with a groan of anguish, and buried his face in his pillow.

Miss Marilla paused in horror, thinking she had intruded upon some secret meditation; but, as she waited on tiptoe and breathless in the hall, she heard the steady hoarse breathing keep on, and knew that he was still asleep. He did not rouse, more than to open bloodshot, unseeing eyes and close them again when she loudly stirred his medicine in the glass and held the spoon to his lips. As before, he obediently opened his mouth and swallowed, and went on sleeping.

She stood a moment anxiously watching him. She did not know just what she ought to do. Perhaps he was going to have pneumonia! Perhaps she ought to send for the doctor, and yet there

were complications about that. She
would be obliged to explain a lot—or
else lie to the neighborhood! And he
might not like it for her to call a doctor
while he was asleep. If she only had
some one with whom to advise! On or-
dinary questions she always consulted
Mary Amber, but by the very nature
of the case Mary Amber was out of
this. Besides, in half an hour Mary
Amber very discreetly put herself beyond a question outside of any touch
with Miss Marilla's visitor by taking
herself off in her little runabout for a
short visit to a college friend over in the
next county. It was plain that Mary
Amber did not care to subject herself
to further contact with the young soldier. He might be Dick or he might
not be Dick. It was none of her business while she was visiting Jeannette
Clark; so she went away quite hurriedly.
Miss Marilla heard the purr of the

engine as the little brown car started down the hedged driveway, and watched the flight with a sense of satisfaction. She had an intuition that Mary Amber was not in favor of her soldier, and she had a guilty sense of hiding the truth from her dear young friend that made her breathe more freely as she watched Mary Amber's flight. Moreover, it was with a certain self-reproachful relief that she noted the little brown suitcase that lay at Mary Amber's feet as she slid past Miss Marilla's house without looking up. Mary Amber was going away for the day at least, probably overnight; and by that time the question of the soldier would be settled one way or the other without Mary Amber's having to worry about it.

Miss Marilla ordered a piece of beef, and brewed a cup of the most delicious beef-tea, which she took up-stairs. She

managed to get her soldier awake
enough to swallow it; but it was plain
that he did not in the least realize
where he was, and seemed well content
to close his eyes and drowse away once
more. Miss Marilla was deeply troubled. Some pricks from the old, time-
worn adage beginning, "O what a tang-
led web we weave," began to stab her
conscience. If only she had not allowed
those paragraphs to go into the county
paper! No, that was not the real
trouble at all. If only she had not
dragged in another soldier, and made
Mary Amber believe he was her
nephew! Such an old fool! Just because she couldn't bear the mortification
of having people know her nephew
hadn't cared enough for her to come and
see her when he was close at hand! But
she was well punished. Here she had a
strange sick man on her hands, and no

end of responsibility! Oh, if only she
hadn't asked him in!

Yet, as she stood watching the quick
little throb in his neck above the old
flannel nightgown, and the long, curly
sweep of the dark lashes on his hot
cheek as he slept, her heart cried out
against that wish. No, a thousand
times no. If she had not asked him in,
he might have been in some hospital by
this time, cared for by strangers; and
she would have been alone, with empty
hands, getting her own solitary dinner,
or sewing on the aprons for the orphan-
age, with nothing in the world to do
that really mattered for anybody.
Somehow her heart went out to this
stranger boy with a great yearning, and
he had come to mean her own—or
what her own ought to have been to her.
She wouldn't have him otherwhere for
anything. She wanted him right where
he was for her to care for, something at

last that needed her, something she could love and tend, even if it were only for a few days.

And she was sure she could care for him. She knew a lot about sickness. People sent for her to help them out, and her wonderful nursing had often saved a life where the doctor's remedies had failed. She felt sure this was only a severe case of grippe that had taken fierce hold on the system. Thorough rest, careful nursing, nourishing broth, and some of her homeopathic remedies would work the charm. She would try it a little longer and see. If his temperature wasn't higher than the last time, it would be perfectly safe to get along without a doctor.

She put the thermometer between his relaxed lips, and held them firmly round it until she was sure it had been there long enough. Then she carried it softly over to the front window, and studied it. No, it had not risen; in fact, it might be a fifth of a degree lower.

Well, she would venture it a little while longer.

For two days Miss Marilla cared for her strange soldier as only a born nurse like herself could care, and on the third morning he rewarded her by opening his eyes and looking about; then, meeting her own anxious gaze, he gave her a weak smile.

"I've been sick!" he said as if stating an astonishing fact to himself. "I must have given you a lot of trouble."

"Not a bit of it, you dear child," said Miss Marilla, and then stooped and brushed his forehead with her lips in a motherly kiss. "I'm so glad you're better!"

She passed her hand like soft old fallen rose-leaves over his forehead, and it was moist. She felt of his hands, and they were moist too. She took his temperature, and it had gone down almost to normal. Her eyes were shining with more than professional joy and relief. He had become to her in these hours of nursing and anxiety as her own child.

But at the kiss the boy's eyelashes had swept down upon his cheek; and, when she looked up from reading the thermometer, she saw a tear glisten unwillingly beneath the lashes.

The next two days were a time of untold joy to Miss Marilla while she petted and nursed her soldier boy back to some degree of his normal strength. She treated him just as if he were a little child who had dropped from the skies to her loving ministrations. She bathed his face, and puffed up his pillows, and took his temperature, and dosed him, and fed him, and read him to sleep—and Miss Marilla could read well, too; she was always asked to read the chapter at the Fortnightly Club whenever the regular reader whose turn it was failed. And while he was asleep she cooked dainty, appetizing little dishes for him. They had a wonderful time together, and he enjoyed it as much as she did. The fact was he was too weak to object, for the little red devils that get into the blood and kick up the fight commonly entitled grippe had done a thorough work with him; and he was, as he put it, "all in and *then* some."

He seemed to have gone back to the days of his childhood since the fever began to abate, and he lay in a sweet daze of comfort and rest. His troubles and perplexities and loneliness had dropped away from him, and he felt no desire to think of them. He was having the time of his life.

Then suddenly, wholly unannounced and not altogether desired at the present stage of the game, Mary Amber arrived on the scene.

CHAPTER V

MARY was radiant as the sunny morning in a little red tam, and her cheeks as red as her hat from the drive across country. She appeared at the kitchen door quite in her accustomed way just as Miss Marilla was lifting the dainty tray to carry her boy's breakfast up-stairs, and she almost dropped it in her dismay.

"I've had the grandest time!" breezed Mary gayly. "You don't know how beautiful the country is, all wonderful bronze and brown with a purple haze, and a frost like silver lace this morning when I started. You've simply got to put on your wraps and come with me for a little while. I know a place where the shadows melt slowly, and the frost will not be gone yet. Come quick! I want you to see it be-

fore it's too late. You're not just eating your breakfast, Auntie Rill! And
on a tray, too! Are you sick?"

Miss Marilla glanced guiltily down
at the tray, too transparent even to
evade the question.

"No, why—I—he—my neph——"
then she stopped in hopeless confusion,
remembering her resolve not to tell a
lie about the matter, whatever came.

Mary Amber stood up and looked at
her, her keen young eyes searching and
finding the truth.

"You don't mean to tell me *that man*
is here yet? And you waiting on him!"

There were both sorrow and scorn in
the fine young voice.

In the upper hall the sick soldier in a
bathrobe was hanging over the banisters in a panic, wishing some kind fairy
would arrive and waft him away on a
breath. All his perfidy in getting sick
on a strange gentlewoman's hands and

lying lazily in bed, letting her wait on him, was shown up in Mary Amber's voice. It found its echo in his own strong soul. He had known all along that he had no business there, that he ought to have gone out on the road to die rather than betray the sweet hospitality of Miss Marilla by allowing himself to be a selfish, lazy slob—that was what he called himself as he hung over the banisters.

"Mary! Why, he has been very *sick!*"

"Sick?" There was a covert sneer in Mary Amber's incredulous young voice; and then the conversation was suddenly blanketed by the closing of the hall door, and the sick soldier padded disconsolately back to bed, weak and dizzy, but determined. This was as good a time as any. He ought to have gone before!

He trailed across the room in the big

flannel nightgown that hung out from
him with the outlines of a fat old auntie
and dragged down from one bronzed
shoulder rakishly. His hair was sticking up wildly, and he felt of his chin
fiercely, and realized that he was wear-
ing a growth of several days.

In a neat pile on a chair he found his
few clean garments, and struggled into
them. His carefully ironed uniform
hung in the closet; and he braced himself, and struggled into the trousers. It
seemed a tremendous effort. He longed
to drop back on the pillows, but
wouldn't. He sat with his head in his
hands, his elbows on his knees, trying
to get courage to totter to the bathroom
and subdue his hair and beard, when he
heard Miss Marilla coming hastily up
the stairs, the little coffee-pot sending
on a delicious odor, and the glass of milk
tinkling against the silver spoons as
she came.

He had managed his leggings by this time, and looked up with an attempt at a smile, trying to pass it off in a jocular way.

"I thought it was high time I was getting about," he said, and broke down coughing.

Miss Marilla paused in distress, and looked at his hollow eyes. Everything seemed to be going wrong this morning. Oh, why hadn't Mary Amber stayed away just one day longer? But of course he had not heard her.

"Oh, you're not fit to be up yet!" she exclaimed. "Do lie down and rest till you've had your breakfast."

"I can't be a baby having you wait on me any longer," he said. "I'm ashamed of myself. I ought not to have stayed here at all!" His tone was savage, and he reached for his coat, and jammed it on with a determined air in spite of his weakness and the sore shivers that crept shakily up his back. "I'm perfectly all right, and you've been wonderful; but it's time I was moving on."

He pushed past her hurriedly to the bathroom, feeling that he must get out of her sight before his head began to swim. The water on his face would steady him. He dashed it on, and shivered sickly, longing to plunge back to bed, yet keeping on with his ablutions.

Miss Marilla put down her tray, and stood with tears in her eyes, waiting for him to return, trying to think what she could say to persuade him back to bed again.

Her anxious expression softened him when he came back, and he agreed to eat his breakfast before he went anywhere, and sank gratefully into the big chair in front of the Franklin heater, where she had laid out his breakfast on a little table. She had lined the chair

with a big comfortable, which she drew
unobtrusively about his shoulders now,
slipping a cushion under his feet, and
quietly coddling him into comfort again.
He looked at her gratefully, and, setting down his coffee-cup, reached out
and patted her hair as she rose from
tucking up his feet.

"You're just like a mother to me!"
he choked, trying to keep back the
emotion from his voice. "It's been
great! I can't tell you!"

"You've been just like a dear son,"
she beamed, touching the dark hair
over his forehead shyly. "It's like getting my own back again to have you
come for this little while, and to be able
to do for you. You see it wasn't as if I
really had anybody. Dick never cared
for me. I used to hope he would when
he grew up. I used to think of him
over there in danger, and pray for him,
and love him, and send him sweaters;

7

but now I know it was really you I
thought of and prayed for. Dick never
cared."

He looked at her tenderly, and
pressed her hand gratefully.

"You're wonderful!" he said. "I
shall never forget it."

That little precious time while he was
eating his breakfast made it all the
harder for what he meant to do. He saw
that he could never hope to do it openly,
either; for she would fling herself in
his path to prevent him from going out
until he was well; so he let her tuck him
up carefully on the spread-up bed, and
pull down the shades for him to take a
nap after the exertion of getting
dressed; and he caught her hand, and
kissed it fervently as she was leaving
him; and cherished her murmured
"Dear child!" and the pressure of her
old-rose-leaf fingers in parting. Then
he closed his eyes, and let her slip away

to the kitchen where he knew she would
be some time preparing something
delicious for his dinner.

When she was safely out of hearing,
rattling away at the kitchen stove, he
threw back the covers vigorously, set
his grim determination against the
swimming head, stalked over to the.
little desk, and wrote a note on the fine
note-paper he found there.

"Dear, wonderful little mother," he
wrote, "I can't stay here any longer. It
isn't right. But I'll be back some day
to thank you if everything goes all
right. Sincerely, YOUR BOY."

He tiptoed over, and laid it on the
pillow; then he took his old trench-cap,
which had been nicely pressed and was
hanging on the corner of the looking-
glass, and stealthily slid out of the
pleasant, warm room, down the car-
peted stairs, and out the front door into
the crisp, cold morning. The chill air

met him with a challenge as he closed
the front door, and dared him not to
cough; but with an effort he held his
breath, and crept down the front walk
to the road, holding in control as well
the long, violent shivers that seized him
in their grasp. The sun met him, and
blinded his sensitive eyes; and the wind
with a tang of winter jeered at his thin
uniform, and trickled up his sleeves
and down his collar, penetrating every
seam. But he stuffed his hands into
his pockets, and strode grimly ahead
on the way he had been going when
Miss Marilla met him, passing the tall
hedge where Mary Amber lived, and
trying to hold his head high. He hoped
Mary Amber saw him *going away!*

For perhaps half a mile past Mary
Amber's house his courage and his
pride held him, for he was a soldier,
who had slept in a muck-pile under the
rain, and held his nerve under fire, and

gone on foot ten miles to the hospital
after he was wounded. What was a
little grippe and a walk in the cold to
the neighboring village? He wished
he knew how far it was, but he had to
go, for it would never do to send the
telegram he must send from the town
where Miss Marilla lived.

The second half-mile he lagged and
shivered, with not energy enough to
keep up a circulation; the third half
mile and the fourth were painful, and
the fifth was completed in a sick daze
of weakness; for the cold, though stim-
ulating at first, had been getting in
its work through his uniform, and he
felt chilled to the very soul of him. His
teeth were chattering, and he was blue
around the lips when he staggered into
the telegraph-office of Little Silverton.
His fingers were almost too stiff to
write, and his thoughts seemed to have
congealed also, though he had been re-

peating the message all the way, word for word, with a vague feeling that he might forget it forever if he did not keep it going.

"Will you send that collect?" he asked the operator when he had finished writing.

The girl took the blank, and read it carefully.

" Arthur J. Watkins, Esq.,

   " LaSalle Street, Chicago, Ill.

   " Please negotiate a loan of five hundred dollars for me, using old house as collateral. Wire money immediately Little Silverton. Entirely out of funds. Have been sick.

                              LYMAN GAGE.

The girl read it through again, and then eyed him cautiously.

"What's your address?" she asked, giving a slow speculative chew to her gum.

"I'll wait here," said the big blue soldier, sinking into a rush-bottomed chair by the desk.

"It might be some wait," said the girl dryly, giving him another curious "once-over."

"I'll wait!" he repeated fiercely, and dropped his aching head into his hands.

The little instrument clicked away vigorously. In his fevered brain he fancied it writing on a typewriter at the other end of the line, and felt a curious impatience for his lawyer to read it and reply. How he wished it would hurry!

The morning droned on, the telegraph instrument chattered breezily, with the monotony of a sunny child that knows no larger world and is happy. Sometimes it seemed to Gage as if every click pierced his head and he was going crazy. The shivers were keeping in time running up and down his back, and chilling his very heart. The room was cold, cold, *cold!* How did that fool of a girl stand it in a pink trans-

parent blouse, showing her fat arms
huskily? He shivered. Oh, for one
of Miss Marilla's nice thick blankets,
and a hot-water bag! Oh, for the soft,
warm bed, the quiet room, and Miss
Marilla keeping guard! But he was a
man—and a soldier! And every now
and then would come Mary Amber's
keen accusing voice: "*Is that man* here
yet? And you *waiting on him!*" It
was that that kept him up when he
might have given way. He *must* show
her he was a man, after all. "*That
man!*" What had she meant? Did
she, then, suspect him of being a fraud
and not the real nephew? Well—
shiver, shiver—what did he care? Let
Mary Amber go to thunder! Or, if
she didn't want to go, he would go to
thunder himself. He felt himself there
already.

Two hours went by. Now and then
some one came in with a message, and

went out again. The girl behind the
desk got out a pink sweater she was
knitting, and chewed gum in time to
her needles. Sometimes she eyed her
companion curiously, but he did not
stir nor look up. If there hadn't been
prohibition, she might have thought him
drunk. She began to think about his
message and weave a crude little romance around him. She wondered
whether he had been wounded. If he
had given her half a chance, she would
have asked him questions; but he sat
there with his head in his hands like a
stone image, and never seemed to know
she was in the room. After a while it
got on her nerves; and she took up her
telephone, and carried on a gallery conversation with a fellow laborer somewhere up the line, giggling a good deal
and telling about a movie she went to
the night before. She used rare slang,
with a furtive glance at the soldier for

developments; but he did not stir. Finally she remarked loudly that it was
getting noontime, and "so-longed" her
friend, clicking the receiver into place.

"I gotta go to lunch now," she remarked in an impersonal tone. "I have
a nour off. This office is closed all
noontime."

He did not seem to hear her; so she
repeated it, and Gage looked up with
bloodshot, heavy eyes.

"What becomes of the message if it
comes while you're away?" he asked
feverishly.

"Oh, it'll be repeated," she replied
easily. "You c'n cumbback bime-by,
'bout two o'clock er later, 'n' mebbe
it'll be here. I gotta lock up now."

Lyman Gage dragged himself to his
feet, and looked dazedly about him;
then he staggered out on the street.

The sun hit him a clip in the eyes
again that made him sick, and the wind

caught at his sleeves, and ran down his
collar gleefully. The girl shut the door
with a click, and turned the key, eyeing
him doubtfully. He seemed to her very
stupid for a soldier. If he had given her
half a chance, she would have been
friendly to him. She watched him drag
down the street with an amused contempt, then turned to her belated lunch.

Lyman Gage walked on down the
road a little way, and then began to feel
as if he couldn't stand the cold a second
longer, though he knew he must. His
heart was behaving queerly, seeming to
be absent from his body for whole sec-
onds at a time, and then returning with
leaps and bounds that almost suffocated
him. He paused and looked around for
a place to sit down, and, finding none,
dropped down on the frozen ground at
the roadside. It occurred to him that he
ought to go back now while he was able,

for he was fast getting where from sheer weakness he couldn't walk.

He rested a moment, and then stumbled up and back toward Little Silverton. Automobiles passed him, and he remembered thinking that, if he weren't so sick and queer in his head, he would try to stand in the road and stop one, and get them to carry him somewhere. He had often done that in France, or even in this country during the war. But just now it seemed that he couldn't do that, either. He had set out to prove to Mary Amber that he was a man and a soldier, and holding up automobiles wouldn't be compatible with that idea. Then he realized that all this was crazy thinking, that Mary Amber had gone to thunder, and so had he, and it didn't matter, anyway. All that mattered was for him to get that money and go back and pay Miss Marilla for taking care of him; and then for him to take the next train back to the city, and get to a hospital. If he could only hold out long enough for that. But things were fast getting away from him. His head was hot and in a whirl, and his feet were so cold he thought they must be dead.

Without realizing it he walked by the telegraph-office and on down the road toward Purling Brook again.

The telegraph-girl watched him from the window of the tiny bakery where she ate her lunch.

"There goes that poor boob *now!*" she said with her mouthful of pie a la mode. "He gets my goat! I hope he doesn't come back. He'll never get no answer to that telegram he sent. People ain't goin' round pickin' up five hundred dollarses to send to broke soldiers these days. They got 'um all in Liberty Bonds. Say, Jess, gimme one more o'

them chocolate éclairs, won't you? I
gotta get back."

About that time Lyman Gage had
found a log by the wayside, and sunk
down permanently upon it. He had
no more breath to carry him on, and no
more ambition. If Mary Amber had
gone to thunder, why should he care
whether he got an answer to his telegram or not? She was only another
girl, anyway, GIRL, his enemy! And
he sank into a blue stupor, with his
elbows on his cold, cold knees and his
face hidden in his hands. He had forgotten the shivers now. They had
taken possession of him, and made him
one with them. It might be, after all,
that he was too hot and not too cold;
and there was a strange burning pain in
his chest when he tried to breathe, so he
wouldn't breathe. What was the use?

CHAPTER VI

MISS MARILLA tiptoed softly up the hall, and listened at the door of the spare bedroom. It was time her soldier-boy woke up and had some dinner. She had a beautiful little treat for him to-day, chicken broth with rice, and some little bits of tender breast-meat on toast, with a quivering spoonful of currant jelly.

It was very still in the spare room, so still that a falling coal from the grate of the Franklin heater made a hollow sound when it fell into the pan below. If the boy was asleep, she could usually tell by his regular breathing; but, though she listened with a keen ear, she could not hear it to-day. Perhaps he was awake, sitting up. She pushed the door open, and looked in. Why! The bed was empty! She glanced around the room, and *it was empty too!*

She passed her hand across her eyes as if they had deceived her, and went over to look at the bed. Surely he must be there somewhere! And then she saw the note.

"Dear wonderful little mother!"

Her eyes were too blurred with quick tears and apprehension to read any further. "Mother!" He had called her that. She could never feel quite alone in the world again. But where was he? She took the corner of her white apron, and wiped the tears away vigorously to finish the note. Then, without pausing to think, and even in the midst of her great gasp of apprehension, she turned swiftly, and went down-stairs, out the front door, across the frozen lawn, and through the hedge to Mary Amber's house.

"Mary! Mary Amber!" she called as she panted up the steps, the note grasped tightly in her trembling hand. She hoped, oh, she hoped Mary Amber's mother would not come to the door and ask questions. Mary's mother was so sensible, and Miss Marilla always felt as if Mrs. Amber disapproved of her just a little whenever she was doing anything for anybody. Not that Mary Ambers' mother was not kind herself to people, but she was always so very sensible in her kindness, and did things in the regular way, and wasn't impulsive like Miss Marilla.

But Mary Amber herself came to the door, with pleasant forgetfulness of her old friend's recent coolness, and tried to draw her into the hall. This Miss Marilla firmly declined, however. She threw her apron over her head and shoulders as a concession to Mary's fears for her health, and broke out:

8

"Oh, don't talk about me, Mary. Talk about *him*. He's gone! I thought he was asleep; and I went up to see if he was ready for his dinner, and he's *gone!* And he's sick, Mary. He's not able to stand up. Why, he's had a fever. It was a hundred and three for two days, and only got down to below normal this morning for the first time. He isn't fit to be out, either, and that little thin uniform with no overcoat!"

The tears were streaming down Miss Marilla's sweet Dresden-china face, and Mary Amber's heart was touched in spite of her.

She came and put her arm around Miss Marilla's shoulder, and drew her down the steps and over to her own home, closing the door carefully first so that her mother need not be troubled about it. Mary Amber always had tact when she wanted to use it.

"Where was he going, dear?" she asked sympathetically, with a view to making out a good case for the soldier without Miss Marilla's bothering further about him.

"I—do-don't know!" sobbed Miss Marilla. "He just thought he ought not to stay and bother me. Here! See his note."

"Well, I'm glad he had some sense," said Mary Amber with satisfaction. "He was perfectly right about not staying to bother you." She took the little crumpled note and smoothed it out.

"O my dear, you don't understand," sobbed Miss Marilla. "He's been such a good, dear boy, and so ashamed he had troubled me! And really, Mary, he'll not be able to stand it. Why, you ought to see how little clothes he had! So thin, and cotton underwear! I washed them and mended them, but he ought to have had an overcoat."

"Oh, well, he'll go to the city and get something warm, and go to a hospital if he feels sick," said Mary Amber comfortably. "I wouldn't worry about him. He's a soldier. He's stood lots worse things than a little cold. He'll look out for himself."

"Don't!" said Miss Marilla fiercely. "Don't say that, Mary! You don't understand. He is *sick,* and he's all the soldier-boy I've got; and I've *got* to go after him. He can't be gone very far, and he really isn't able to walk. He's weak. I just can't stand it to have him go this way."

Mary Amber looked at her with a curious light in her eyes.

"And yet, Auntie Rill, you know it was fine of him to do it," she said with a dancing dimple in the corner of her mouth. "Well, I see what you want; and, much as I hate to, I'll take my car and scour the country for him. What time did you say he left?"

"O Mary Amber!" smiled Miss Marilla through her tears. "You're a good girl. I knew you'd help me. I'm sure you can find him if you try. He can't have been gone over an hour, not much; for I've only fixed the chicken and put my bread in the pans since I left him."

"I suppose he went back to the village, but there hasn't been any train since ten, and you say he was still there at ten. He's likely waiting at the station for the twelve o'clock. I'll speed up and get there before it comes. I have fifteen minutes. I"—glancing at her wrist-watch—"I guess I can make it."

"I'm not so sure he went that way," said Miss Marilla, looking up the road past Mary Amber's house. "He was on his way up that way when—" and then Miss Marilla suddenly shut her mouth, and did not finish the sentence. Mary Amber gave her another curious, discerning look, and nodded brightly.

"You go in and get warm, Auntie Rill. Leave that soldier to me; I'll bring him home." Then she sped back through the hedge to the little garage, and in a few minutes was speeding down the road toward the station. Miss Marilla watched her in troubled silence, and then, putting on her cape that always hung handy by the hall-door, walked a little distance up the road, straining her old eyes, but seeing nothing. Finally in despair she turned back; and presently, just as she reached her own steps again, she saw Mary's car come flying back with only Mary in it. But Mary did not stop nor even look toward the house. She sped on up the road this time, and the purring of the engine was sweet music to Miss Ma-

rilla's ears. Dear Mary Amber, how
she loved her!

* * *

The big blue soldier, cold to the soul
of him, and full of pain that reminded
him of the long horror of the war, was
still sitting by the roadside with his head
in his hands when Mary Amber's car
came flying down the road. She stopped before him with a little triumphant
purr of the engine, so close to him that
it roused him from his lethargy to
look up.

"I should think you'd be ashamed of
yourself, running away from Miss Marilla like this, and making her worry
herself sick!" Mary Amber's voice was
keen as icicles, and the words went
through him like red-hot needles. He
straightened up, and the light of battle
came back to his eyes. This was GIRL
again, his enemy. His firm upper lip
moved sensitively, and came down

straight and strong against the lower
one, showing the nice line of character
that made his mouth beautiful.

"Thank you," he said coldly. "I'm
only ashamed that I stayed so long."
His tone further added that he did not
know what business of hers it was.

"Well, she sent me for you; and you'll
please to get in quickly, for she's very
much worked up about you."

Mary Amber's tone stated that she
herself was not in the least worked up
about a great, hulking soldier that
would let a woman wait on him for several days hand and foot, and then run
away when her back was turned.

"Kindly tell her that I am sorry I
troubled her, but that it is not possible
for me to return at present," he answered stiffly. "I came down to send
a business telegram, and I am waiting
for an answer."

A sudden shiver seized him, and rippled involuntarily over his big frame. Mary Amber was eying him contemptuously, but a light of pity stole into her eyes as she saw him shiver.

"You are cold!" said Mary Amber as if she were charging him with an offence.

"Well, that's not strange—is it—on a day like this? I haven't made connections yet with an overcoat and gloves; that's all."

"Look here; if you are cold, you've simply got to get into this car and let me take you back to Miss Marilla. You'll catch your death of cold sitting there like that."

"Well, I may be cold; but I don't *have* to let you take me anywhere. When I get ready to go, I'll walk. As for catching my death of cold, that's strictly my own affair. There's nobody in the world would care if I did."

The soldier had blue lights like steel in his eyes, and his mouth looked very soldier-like indeed. His whole manner showed that there wasn't the least use in the world trying to argue with him.

Mary Amber eyed him with increasing interest and thoughtfulness.

"You're mistaken," she said grudgingly. "There's one. There's Miss Marilla. She'd break her heart. She's like that; and she hasn't much to care for in the world, either. Which makes it all the worse what you've done. Oh, I don't see how you *could* deceive her."

"Deceive her?" said the astonished soldier. "I never deceived her."

"Why, you let her think you were Dick Chadwick, her nephew; and you *know* you're not! *I* knew you weren't the minute I saw you, even before I found Dick's telegram in the stove saying he couldn't come. And then I asked you a lot of questions to find out

for sure, and you couldn't answer one
of them right." Her eyes were spark-
ling, and there was an eager look in her
face, like an appeal, almost as if she
wanted him to prove what she was saying was not true.

"No, I'm not Dick Chadwick," said
the young man with fine dignity. "But
I never deceived Miss Marilla."

"Well, who did then?" There were
disappointment and unbelief in Mary
Amber's voice.

"Nobody. She isn't deceived. It
was she who tried to deceive you."

"What do you mean?"

"I mean she wanted you to think I
was her nephew. She was mortified, I
guess, because he didn't turn up, and
she didn't want you to know. So she
asked me to dinner to fill in. I didn't
know anybody was there till just as I
was going in the door. Then I had to
go and get sick in the night, and dish

the whole thing. I was a fool to give
in to her, of course, and stay that night,
but it did sound good to have a real
night's sleep in a bed. I didn't think
I was such a softie as to get out of my
head and be on her hands like that. But
you needn't worry. I intend to make
it up to her fully just as soon as I can
lay hands on some funds—"

He suddenly broke into a fit of
coughing so hoarse and croupy as to
alarm even Mary Amber's cool contempt. She reached back in the car,
and, grasping a big fur coat, sprang out
on the hard ground, and threw the coat
about him, tucking it around his neck
and trying to fasten a button under his
chin against his violent protest.

"You're very kind," he gasped
loftily, as soon as he could recover his
breath. "But I can't put that on, and
I'm going down to the telegraph-office
now to see if my wire has come yet."

"Look here," said Mary Amber in quite a different tone, "I'm sorry I was so suspicious. I see I didn't understand. I ask your pardon, and won't you please put on this coat, and get into this car, and let me take you home quick? I'm really very much troubled about you."

The soldier looked up in surprise at the gentleness, and almost his heart melted. The snarly look around his mouth and eyes disappeared, and he seemed a bit confounded.

"Thank you," he said simply. "I appreciate that. But I can't let you help me, you know."

"Oh, please!" she said, a kind of little-girl alarm springing into her eyes. "I sha'n't know what to say to Miss Marilla. I promised her to bring you back, you know."

His eyes and lips were hardening again. She saw he did not mean to yield, and Mary Amber was not used to being balked in her purposes. She glanced down the road; and a sudden light came into her eyes, and brought a dimple of mischief into her cheek.

"You'll have to for my sake," she said hurriedly in a lower tone. "There's a car coming with some people in it I know; and they will think it awfully queer for me to be standing here on a lonely roadside talking to a strange soldier sitting on a log on a day like this. Hurry!"

Lyman Gage glanced up, saw the car coming swiftly; saw, too, the dimple of mischief; but with an answering light of gallantry in his own eyes he sprang up and helped her into the car. The effort brought on another fit of coughing, but as soon as he could speak he said:

"You can take me down to that little telegraph-office if you please, and drop

me there. Then nobody will think anything about it."

"I'll take you to the telegraph-office
if you'll be good and put that coat on
right, and button it," said Mary Amber
commandingly. She had him in the
car now, and she knew that she could
go so fast he could not get out. "But
I shall not stop there until you promise
me on your honor as a soldier that you
will not get out or make any more
trouble about my taking you back to
Miss Marilla."

The soldier looked very balky indeed,
and his firm mouth got itself into fine
shape again, till he looked into Mary
Amber's eyes and saw the saucy, beautiful lights there; and then he broke
down laughing.

"Well, you've caught me by guile,"
he said; "and I guess we're about even.
I'll go back and make my adieus myself to Miss Marilla."

A little curve of satisfaction settled about Mary Amber's mouth.

"Put that coat on, please," she said, and the soldier put it on gratefully. He was beginning to feel a reaction from his battle with Mary Amber, and now that he was defeated the coat seemed most desirable.

"Don't you think it would be a good idea if you would tell me who you really are?" asked Mary Amber. "It might save some embarrassment."

"Why, certainly!" said the soldier in surprise. "It hadn't occurred to me; that's all. I'm Lyman Gage, of Chicago." He named also his rank and regiment in the army. Then, looking at her curiously, he said, hesitating:

"I'm—perfectly respectable, you know. I don't really make a practice of going around sponging on unprotected ladies."

Her cheeks flamed a gorgeous scarlet, and her eyes looked rebuked.

"I suppose I ought to apologize," she said. "But really, you know, it looked rather peculiar to me—" She stopped suddenly, for he was seized with another fit of coughing, which had so shrill a sound that she involuntarily turned to look at him with anxious eyes.

"I s'pose it did look queer," he managed to say at last; "but you know that day when I came in I didn't care a hang." He dropped his head wearily against the car, and closed his eyes for just a second, as if the keeping of them open was a great effort.

"You're all in now!" she said sharply. "And you're shivering! You ought to be in bed this minute." Her voice held deep concern. "Where is that telegraph-office? We'll just leave word for them to forward the message if it hasn't come and then we'll fly back."

"Oh, I must wait for that message," he said, straightening up with a hoarse effort and opening his eyes sharply. "It is really imperative."

She stopped the car in front of the telegraph-office. The little operator, scenting a romance, scuttled out of the door with an envelope in her hand and a different look on her face from the one she had worn when she went to her lunch. To tell the truth, she had not had much faith in that soldier nor in the message he had sent "collect." She hadn't believed any answer would come, or at least any favorable one.

Now she hurried across the pavement to the car, studying Mary Amber's red tam as she talked, and wondering whether she couldn't make one like it out of the red lining of an old army cape she had.

"Yer message's come," she announced affably. "Come just after I

got back. An' I got yer check all made
out fer yah. You sign here. See? Got
anybody to 'dentify yah? 'Tain't necessary, see? I c'n waive identification."

"I can identify him," spoke up Mary
Amber with cool dignity; and the soldier looked at her wonderingly. That
was a very different tone from the one
she had used when she came after him.
After all, what did Mary Amber know
about him?

He looked at the check half wonderingly as if it were not real. His head
felt very queer. The words of the message seemed all jumbled. He crumpled
it in his hand.

"Ain't yah going to send an answer?"
put in the little operator aggrievedly,
hugging the thin muslin sleeves of her
little soiled shirt-waist to keep from
shivering. "He says to wire him immediately. He says it's important. I

guess you didn't take notice to the message."

The soldier tried to smooth out the crumpled paper with his numb fingers; and Mary Amber, seeing that he was feeling very miserable, took it from him, and capably put it before him.

"Am sending you a thousand. Wire me your post-office address immediately. Good news. Important.

"(Signed)
"ARTHUR J. WATKINS."

"I guess I can't answer that now," said the soldier, trying his best to keep his teeth from chattering. "I don't just know—"

"Here, I'll write it for you," said Mary with sudden understanding. "You better have it sent in Aunt Rill's care; and then you can ¹..ve it forwarded anywhere, you know. I'll write it for you;" and she took a silver pencil from the pocket of her coat, and wrote the telegram rapidly on a corner she tore from the first message, handing it out for his inspection and then passing it on to the operator, who gathered it in capably.

"Send this c'lect too, I s'pose," she called after the car as it departed.

"Yes, all right, anything," answered Lyman Gage, wearily sinking back in the seat. "It doesn't matter, anyway."

"You are sick!" said Mary Amber anxiously; "and we are going to get right home. Miss Marilla will be wild."

The soldier sat up holding his precious check.

"I'll have to ask you to let me out," he said, trying to be dignified under the heavy stupor of weariness that was creeping over him. "I've got to get to a bank."

"Oh, must you, to-day? Couldn't we wait till to-morrow or till you feel better?" asked Mary anxiously.

"No, I must go now," he insisted doggedly.

"Well, there's a bank on the next corner," she said; "and it must be about closing-time." She shoved her sleeve back, and glanced at her watch. "Just five minutes of three. We'll stop, but you'll promise to hurry, won't you? I want to get you home. I'm worried about you."

Lyman Gage cast her another of those wondering looks like a child unused to kindness suddenly being petted. It made her feel as if she wanted to cry. All the mother in her came to her eyes. She drew up in front of the bank, and got out after him.

"I'll go in with you," she said. "They know me over here, and it may save you trouble."

"You're very kind," he said almost curtly. "I dislike to make you so much trouble——"

Perhaps it was owing to Mary's

presence that the transaction went through without question, and in a few minutes more they were back in the car again, Mary tucking up her big patient fussily.

"You're going to put this around your neck," she said, drawing a bright woolly scarf from her capacious coat-pocket, "and around your head," she added, drawing a fold comfortingly up around his ears and the back of his head. "And keep it over your nose and mouth. Breathe through it; don't let this cold air get into your lungs," she finished with a businesslike air as if she were a nurse.

She drew the ends of the scarf around, completely hiding everything but his eyes, and tucked the ends into the neck of the fur coat. Then she produced another lap-robe from some region beneath her feet, and tucked that carefully around him. It was wonderful being taken care of in this way; if

he only had not been so cold, so tired,
and so sore all over he could have enjoyed it. The scarf had a delicate
aroma of spring and violets, something
that reminded him of pleasant things in
the past; but it all seemed like a dream.

They were skimming along over the
road up which he had come at so labo-
rious a pace, and the icy wind cut his
eyeballs. He closed his eyes, and a hot
curtain seemed to shut him out from a
weary world. Almost he seemed to be
spinning away into space. He tried to
open his mouth under the woollen fragrance and speak; but his companion
ordered him sharply to be still till he
got where it was warm, and a sharp
cough like a knife caught him. So he
sank back again into the perfumed
silence of the fierce heat and cold that
seemed to be raging through his body,
and continued the struggle to keep from
drifting into space. It did not seem
quite gallant or gentlemanly to say

nothing, nor soldierly to drift away like that when she was being so kind. And then a curious memory of the other girl drifted around in the frost of his breath mockingly, as if she were laughing at his situation, almost as if she had put him there and was glad. He tried to shake this off by opening his eyes and concentrating them on Mary Amber as she sat sternly at her wheel, driving her little machine for all it was worth, her eyes anxious, and the flush on her cheek bright and glowing. The fancy came to him that she was in league with him against the other girl. He knew it was foolish, and he tried to drive the idea away; but it stayed till she passed her own hedge and stopped the car at Miss Marilla's gate.

Then it seemed to clear away, and common sense reigned for a few brief moments while he stumbled out of the car and staggered into Miss Marilla's parlor and into the warmth and cheer of that good woman's almost tearful, affectionate welcome.

"I want you to take that," he said, hoarsely pressing into her hand the roll of bills he had got at the bank; and then he slid down into a big chair, and everything whirled away again.

Miss Marilla stood aghast, looking at the money and then at the sick soldier, till Mary Amber took command. He never remembered just what happened, nor knew how he got up-stairs and into the great warm, kind bed again, with hot-broth being fed him, and hot-water bags in places needing them. He did not hear them call the doctor on the telephone, nor know just when Mary Amber slipped away down to her car again and rode away.

But Mary Amber knew that this was the afternoon when *The Purling Brook Chronicle* went to press, and she had an item that must get in. Quite demurely she handed the envelope to the woman editor just as she was preparing to mail the last of her copy to the printer in the city. The item read: "Miss Marilla Chadwick, of Shirley Road, is entertaining over the week-end Sergeant Lyman Gage, of Chicago, but just returned from France. Sergeant Gage is a member of the same division and came over in the same ship with Miss Chadwick's nephew, Lieutenant Richard Chadwick, of whom mention has been made in a former number, and has seen long and interesting service abroad."

Mary Amber was back at the house almost before she had been missed and just as the doctor arrived, ready to serve in any capacity whatever.

"Do you think I ought to introduce him to the doctor?" asked Miss Marilla of Mary in an undertone at the head of the stairs, while the doctor was divest-

ing himself of his big fur overcoat. She
had a drawn anxious look like one about
to be found out in a crime.

"He doesn't look to me as if he were
able to acknowledge the introduction,"
said Mary with a glance in at the spare
bed, where the young man lay sleeping
heavily and breathing noisily.

"But—ought I to tell him his name?"

"That's all right, Auntie Rill," said
Mary easily; "I told him his name was
Gage when I phoned, and said he was
in the same division with your nephew.
It isn't necessary for you to say any-
thing about it."

Miss Marilla paused, and eyed Mary
strangely with a frightened, appealing
look, and then with growing relief. So
Mary knew! She sighed, and turned
back to the sick-room with a comforted
expression growing round her mouth.

But the comforted expression
changed once more to anxiety, and self

was forgotten utterly when Miss Marilla began to watch the doctor's face as the examination progressed.

"What has this young man been doing?" he growled, rising from a position on his knees where he had been listening to the soldier's breathing with an ever-increasing frown. Miss Marilla looked at Mary quite frightened, and Mary stepped into the breach.

"He had a heavy cold when he came here, and Miss Chadwick nursed him, and he was doing nicely; but he ran away this morning. He had some business to attend to, and slipped away before anybody could stop him. He got very much chilled, I think."

"I should say he did!" ejaculated the doctor. "Young fool! I suppose he thought he could stand anything because he went through the war. Well, he'll get his now. He's in for pneumonia. I'm sorry, Miss Chadwick, but

I'm afraid you've got a bad case on your hands. Would you like to have me phone for an ambulance and get him to the hospital? I think it can be done at once with a minimum of risk."

"Oh, no, no!" said Miss Marilla, clasping one white hand and then the other nervously. "I couldn't think of that—at least, not unless you think it's necessary—not unless you think it's a risk to stay here. You see he's my— that is, he's almost—like—my own nephew." She lifted appealing eyes.

"Oh, I beg your pardon!" he said with a look of relief. "In that case he's to be congratulated. But, madam, you'll have your hands full before you are through. He's made a very bad start —a very bad start indeed. When these big, husky fellows get sick, they do it thoroughly, you know. Now, if you'll just step over here, Miss Mary, I'll explain to you both about this medicine.

Give this every half-hour till I get back. I'll run up here again in about two hours. I've got to drive over to the Plush Mills now, to an accident case; but I'll be back as quick as I can. I want to watch this fellow pretty closely for the first few hours."

When the doctor was gone, Mary Amber and Miss Marilla stood one on each side of the bed, and looked at each other, making silent covenant together over the sick soldier.

"Now," said Mary Amber softly, "I'm going down into the kitchen to look after things. You just sit here and watch him. I'll run over first to put the car away and tell mother I'll stay with you to-night."

"O Mary Amber, you mustn't do that," said Miss Marilla anxiously. "I never meant to get you into all this scrape. Your mother won't like it at all. I'll get along all right; and any-

way, if I find I can't, I'll get Molly
Poke to come and help me."

"Mother will be perfectly satisfied to
have me help you in any way I can,"
said Mary Amber with a light in her
eyes; "and as for Molly Poke, if I can't
look after you better than she can, I'll
go and hide my head. You can get
Molly Poke when I fail, but not till
then. Now, Auntie Rill, go sit down
in the rockingchair and rest. Didn't I
tell you I'd help get that turkey dinner?
Well, the dinner isn't over yet; that's
all; and I owe the guest an apology for
misjudging him. He's all right, and
we've got to pull him through, Auntie
Rill; so here goes."

Mary Amber gave Miss Marilla a
loving squeeze, and sped down the
stairs. Miss Marilla sat down to listen
to the heavy breathing of the sick soldier, and watch the long, dark lashes on
the sunken, tanned cheeks.

CHAPTER VII

For three weeks the two women nursed Lyman Gage, with now and then the help of Molly Poke in the kitchen. There were days when they came and went silently, looking at each other with stricken glances and at the sick man with pity; and Mary Amber went and looked at the letter lying on the bureau, and wondered whether she ought to telegraph that man who had sent the soldier the money that day. Another letter arrived, and then a telegram, all from Chicago. Then Mary Amber and Miss Marilla talked it over, and decided to make some reply.

By that time the doctor had said that Lyman Gage would pull through; and he had opened his eyes once or twice and smiled weakly upon them. Mary Amber went to the telegraph-office, and sent a message to the person in Chicago whose name was written at the left-hand corner of the envelopes, the same that had been signed to that first telegram.

"Lyman Gage very ill at my home, pneumonia, not able to read letters or telegram. Slight improvement to-day.
"(Signed)
"MARILLA CHADWICK."

Within three hours an answer arrived.

"Much distressed at news of Gage's illness. Cannot come on account of fractured bone, automobile accident. Please keep me informed, and let me know if there is anything I can do.
"(Signed)
"ARTHUR J. WATKINS."

Mary wrote a neat little note that night before she went on duty in the sick-room, stating that the invalid had smiled twice that day and asked what day of the week it was. The doctor felt that he was on the high road to recovery now, and there was nothing to do but be patient. They would show him his mail as soon as the doctor was willing, which would probably be in a few days now.

The day they gave Lyman Gage his mail to read the sun was shining on a new fall of snow, and the air was crisp and clear. There were geraniums blossoming in the spare-room windows between the sheer white curtains, and the Franklin heater was glowing away and filling the place with the warmth of summer.

The patient had been fed what he called "a real breakfast," milk toast and a soft-boiled egg, and the sun was streaming over the foot of the bed gayly as if to welcome him back to life. He seemed so much stronger that the doctor had given permission for him to be bolstered up with an extra pillow while he read his mail.

He had not seemed anxious to read the mail, nor at all curious, even when they told him it was postmarked Chicago. Miss Marilla carried it to him gayly as if she were bringing him a bouquet, but Mary eyed him with a curious misgiving. Perhaps, after all, there would not be good news. He seemed so very apathetic. She watched him furtively as she tidied the room, putting away the soap and towels, and pulling a dry leaf or two from the geraniums. He was so still, and it took him so long to make up his mind to tear open the envelopes after he had them in his thin white hand. It almost seemed as if he dreaded them like a blow, and was trying to summon courage to meet them. Once, as she looked at him, his eye met hers with a deprecatory smile, and to cover her confusion she spoke impulsively.

"You don't seem deeply concerned about the news," she said gayly.

He smiled again almost sadly.

"Well, no!" he said thoughtfully. "I can't say I am. There really isn't anything much left in which to be interested. You see about the worst things that could happen have happened, and there's no chance for anything else."

"You can't always tell," said Mary Amber cheerfully, as she finished dusting the bureau and took herself downstairs for his morning glass of milk and egg.

Slowly Lyman Gage tore the envelope of the topmost letter, and took out the written sheet. In truth he had little curiosity. It was likely an account of how his lawyer friend had paid back the money to Mr. Harrower, or else the details of the loan on the old Chicago house. Houses and loans and such things seemed far from his world just now. He was impatient for Mary Amber to come back with that milk and egg. Not so much for the milk and egg as for the comfort it gave, and the cheeriness of her presence. Presently Miss Marilla would come up and tell over some little incident of Mary's childhood exactly as if he were Dick, the real nephew; and he liked it. Not that he liked Dick, the villain! He found himself hopelessly jealous of him sometimes. Yet he knew in a feeble far-away sense that this was only a foolish foible of an invalid, and he would get over it and laugh at himself when he got well.

He smiled at the pleasantness of it all, this getting-well business, and then turned his indifferent attention to the letter.

"Dear Gage," it read, "what in the world did you hide yourself away in that remote corner of the world for? I've scoured the country to get trace of you without a single result till your telegram came. There's good news to tell you. The unexpected has happened, and you are a rich man, old fellow. Don't let it turn your head, for there's plenty of business to occupy you as soon as you are able to return.

"To make a long story short, the old tract of land in which you put all you had and a good deal more has come to the front in great shape at last. You will remember that the ore was found to be in such shape when they came to the mining of it that it would cost fabulous sums for the initial operations, and it fell through because your company couldn't afford to get the proper machinery. Well, the Government has taken over the whole tract, and is working it. I am enclosing the details on another paper, and you will perceive, when you have looked it over, how very much you are needed at home just now to decide numerous questions which have taxed my ingenuity to the limit to know just what you would want done. There is a great deal of timber on those lands also, very valuable timber, it seems; and that is another source of wealth for you. Oh, this war has been a great thing for you, young man; and you certainly ought to give extra thanks that you came out alive to enjoy it all. Properly managed, your property ought to keep you on Easy Street for the rest of your life, and then some.

"I took pains to let Mr. Harrower know how the wind blew when I paid him the money you had borrowed from him. He certainly was one surprised man; and of course I don't speak officially, but from what he said I should judge that this might make a big difference with Miss Elinore. So you better hurry home, old man, and get busy. The sun is shining, and the war is over.

"Yours fraternally as well as officially,

"ARTHUR J. WATKINS."

Over the first part of the letter Lyman Gage dallied comfortably as he might have done with his grapefruit or the chicken on toast that they had promised him for lunch. He had lost his sense of world values for the time being, and just now a fortune was no more than a hot-water bag when one's feet were cold. It merely gave him a sense that he needn't be in a hurry getting well, that he could take things easy because he could pay for everything and give his friends a good time after he was on his feet again. In short, he was no longer a beggar on Miss Marilla's bounty with only a thousand dollars between him and debt or even the poorhouse.

But, when he came to that last paragraph, his face suddenly hardened, and into his eyes there came a glint of steel as of old, while his jaw set sternly, and

lines came around his mouth, hard, bitter lines.

So it was that that had been the matter with Elinore, was it? She had not
grown tired of *him* so much, but had
wanted more money than she thought
he would be able to furnish for a long
time? He stared off into the room not
seeing its cozy details for the first time
since he began to get well. He was
looking at the vision of the past trying
to conjure up a face whose loveliness
had held for him no imperfections. He
was looking at it squarely now as it
rose dimly in vision against the gray of
Miss Marilla's spare-room wall; and
for the first time he saw the petted
under lip with the selfish droop at its
corners, the pout when she could not
have her own way, the frown of the
delicate brows, the petulant tapping of
a dainty foot, the proud lifted shoulder,
the haughty stare, the cold tones and

crushing contempt that were hers
sometimes. These had seldom been for
him; and, when he had seen them, he
had called them beautiful, had gloried
in them, fool that he was! Why had
he been so blind, when there were girls
in the world like—well—say like Mary
Amber?

Misjudging Elinore? Well, perhaps, but somehow he did not believe
he was. Something had cleared his
vision. He began to remember things
in Elinore Harrower that he had never
called by their true names before. It
appeared more than likely that Elinore
had deliberately left him for a richer
man, and that it was entirely possible
under the changed circumstances that
she might leave the richer man for him
if he could prove that he was the richer
of the two. Bah! What a thing to
get well to! Why did there have to be
things like that in the world? Well, it

mattered very little to him what Elinore did. It might make a difference with her, but it would make no difference to him. There were things in that letter of hers that had cut too deep. He could never forget them, no, never, not even if she came crawling to his feet and begging him to come back to her. As for going back to Chicago, business be hanged! He was going to stay right here and get well. A smile melted out on his lips, and comfort settled down about him as he heard Mary Amber's step on the stairs and the soothing clink of the spoon in the glass of egg and milk.

"Good news?" asked Mary Amber as she shoved up the little serving-table and prepared to administer the egg and milk.

"Oh, so-so!" he answered with a smile, sweeping the letters away from him and looking at the foaming glass with eager eyes.

"Why! You haven't opened them all!" laughed Mary Amber.

"Oh! Haven't I?" he said impatiently, sweeping them up and tearing them open wholesale with only a glance at each, then throwing them back on the coverlet again.

"Nothing but the same old thing. Hounding me back to Chicago," he grinned. "I'm having much too good a time to get well too fast, you may be sure."

Somehow the room seemed cozier after that, and his sleep the sweeter when he took his nap. He ate his chicken on toast slowly to prolong the happy time; and he listened and smiled with deep relish at the little stories Miss Marilla told of Mary Amber's childhood, the gingerbread men with currant eyes, and the naughty Dick who stole them. This world he was in now was such a happy, clean little world,

so simple and so good! Oh, if he could
have known a world like this earlier in
his life! If only he could have been the
hapless Dick in reality!

Molly Poke was established in the
kitchen down-stairs now, and Miss Marilla hovered over her anxiously, leaving the entertaining of the invalid much
to Mary Amber, who wrote neat business letters for him, telling his lawyer
friend to do just as he pleased with
everything till he got back; and who
read stories and bits of poems, and
played chess with him as soon as the
doctor allowed. Oh, they were having
a happy time, the three of them! Miss
Marilla hovered over the two as if they
had been her very own children.

And then one lovely winter afternoon, when they were just discussing
how perhaps they might take the invalid out for a ride in the car some day

next week, the fly dropped into the ointment!

It was as lovely a fly as ever walked on tiny French heels, and came in a limousine lined with gray duvetyn and electrically heated and graced with hothouse rosebuds in a slender glass behind the chauffeur's right ear. She picked her way daintily up the snowy walk, surveyed the house and grounds critically as far as the Amber hedge, and rang the bell peremptorily.

Miss Marilla herself went to the front door, for Molly Poke was busy making cream-puffs and couldn't stop; and, when she saw the little fly standing haughtily on the porch, swathed in a gorgeous moleskin cloak with a voluminous collar of tailless ermine, and a little toque made of coral velvet embroidered in silver, she thought right away of a spider. A very beautiful spider, it is true, but all the same a spider.

And, when the beautiful red lips opened and spoke, she thought so all the more.

"I have come to see Lyman Gage," she announced freezingly, looking at Miss Marilla with the glance one gives to a servant. Miss Marilla cast a frightened glance of discernment over the beautiful little face. For it was beautiful, there was no mistaking that, very perfectly beautiful, though it might have been only superficially so. Miss Marilla was not used to seeing a skin that looked like soft rose-leaves in baby perfection on a person of that age. Great baby eyes of blue, set wide, with curling dark lashes, eyebrows that seemed drawn by a fairy brush, lips of such ruby-red pout, and nose chiselled in warm marble. Peaches and cream floated through her startled mind, and it never occurred to her it was not natural. Oh, the vision was beautiful; there was no doubt about that.

Miss Marilla closed the door, and stood with her back to the stairs and a look of defence upon her face. She had a fleeting thought of Mary and whether she ought to be protected. She had a spasm of fierce jealousy, and a frenzy as to what she should do.

"You can step into the parlor," she said in a tone that she hoped was calm, although she knew it was not cordial. "I'll go up and see if he's able to see you. He's been very sick. The doctor hasn't let him see any"—she paused, and eyed the girl defiantly—"any *strangers.*"

"Oh, that'll be all right," laughed the girl with a disagreeable tinkle. "I'm not a stranger. I'm only his fiancée." But she pronounced "fiancée" in a way that Miss Marilla didn't recognize at

11

all, and she looked at her hard. It
wasn't "wife," anyway; and it hadn't
sounded like "sister" or "cousin." Miss
Marilla looked at the snip—that was
what she began to call her in her mind
—and decided that she didn't want her
to see Lyman Gage at all; but of course
Lyman Gage must be the one to decide
that.

"What did you say your name was?"
she asked bluntly.

For answer the girl brought out a
ridiculous little silk bag with a clatter-
ing clasp and chain, and took therefrom
a tiny gold card-case, from which she
handed Miss Marilla a card. Miss Marilla adjusted her spectacles, and
studied it a moment with one foot on
the lower stairs.

"Well," she said reluctantly, "he
hasn't seen any one yet; but I'll go and
find out if you can see him. You can
sit in the parlor." She waved her hand

again toward the open door, and started up-stairs.

The blood was beating excitedly through her ears, and her heart pounded in pitiful thuds. If this "snip" belonged to her soldier boy, she was sure she could never mother him again. She wouldn't feel at home. And her thoughts were so excited that she did not know that the fur-clad snip was following her close behind until she was actually within the spare bedroom, and holding out the card to her boy with a trembling little withered-rose-leaf hand.

The boy looked up with his wide, pleasant smile like a benediction, and reached out for the card interestedly. He caught the look of panic on Miss Marilla's face and the inscrutable one on Mary Amber's. Mary had heard the strange voice below and arisen from her reading aloud to glance out of the window. She now beat a precipitate retreat into the little sewing-room just off the spare bedroom. Then Lyman Gage realized another presence in the room, and looked beyond to the door where stood Elinore Harrower, her big eyes watching him jealously from her swathing of gorgeous furs, while he slowly took in the situation.

It had been a common saying among his friends that no situation however unexpected ever found Lyman Gage off his guard, or ever saw him give away his own emotions. Like lightning there flitted over his face now a sudden cloud like a curtain, shutting out all that he had been the moment before, putting under lock and seal any like or dislike he might be feeling, allowing only the most cool courtesy to appear in his expression. Miss Marilla, watching him like a cat, could not tell whether he was glad or sorry, surprised or indignant or pleased. He seemed none of these. He glanced with cool indifference toward the lovely vision smiling in the doorway now and ready to gush over him, and a stern dignity grew in the set of his jaws; but otherwise he did not seem to have changed, and most casually, as if he had seen her but the week before, he remarked:

"Oh! Is that you, Elinore? Seems to me you have chosen a cold day to go out. Won't you sit down?" He motioned toward a stiff little chair that stood against the wall, though Mary Amber's rocker was still waving back and forth from her hasty retreat.

Miss Marilla simply faded out of the room, although Gage said politely, "don't leave us, please." But she was gone before the words were out of his mouth, and with a sudden feeling of weakness he glanced around the room wildly, and realized that Mary Amber was gone too.

Mary Amber stood in the sewing-room, and wondered what she ought to do. For the other door of the sewing room was closed and barred by a heavy iron bed that had been put up for convenience during the soldier's illness, and the only spot that was long enough to hold it was straight across the hall door. Obviously Mary Amber could not get out of the sewing-room without moving that bed, and she knew by experience of making it every morning that it squeaked most unmercifully when it was moved. Neither could she go out through the spare bedroom, for she felt that her appearance would cause no end of explanations; and equally of course she dared not shut the door because it would make a noise and call attention to her presence.

So Mary Amber tiptoed softly to the farthest end of the little room, and stood rigidly silent, trying not to listen, yet all the more attuned and sensitive to whatever was going on in the next room. She fairly held her breath lest they should hear her, and pressed her fingers upon her hot eyeballs as if that would shut out the sound.

"That's scarcely the way I expected you to meet me, Lyme," in the sweet lilt of Elinore Harrower's petted voice.

"I was scarcely expecting you, you know, after what has happened," came chillingly in Lyman Gage's voice, a bit high and hollow from his illness, and all the cooler for that.

"I couldn't stay away when I knew you were ill, Lyme, dear!" The voice was honeyed sweet now.

"What had that to do with it?" The tone was almost vicious. "You wrote that we had grown apart, and it was true. You are engaged to another man."

"Well, can't I change my mind?" The

tone was playful, kittenish. It smote
Lyman Gage's memory that he had
been wont to call it teasing and enjoy
it in her once upon a time.

"You've changed your mind once too
often!" The sick man's voice was tense
in his weakness, and his brow was dark.

"Why, Lyme Gage! I think you are
horrid!" cried the girl with a hint of indignant tears in her voice. "Here I
come a long journey to see you when
you're sick; and you meet me that way,
and *taunt* me. It's not like you. You
don't seem a bit glad to see me! Perhaps there's some one else." The voice
had a taunt in it now, and an assurance
that expected to win out in the end, no
matter to what she might have to de-
scend to gain her point.

But she had reckoned without knowl-
edge, for Lyman Gage remembered the
picture he had torn to bits in the dying
light of the sunset and trampled in

the road; those same brilliant eyes, that soft tinted cheek, those painted lips, had smiled impudently up to him that way as he had ground them beneath his heel; and this was GIRL, his natural enemy, who would play with him at her pleasure, and toss him away when he was no longer profitable to her, expecting to find him ready at a word again when circumstances changed. He straightened up with sudden strength, and caught her words with a kind of joyful triumph.

"Yes, there is *some one else!* Mary! Mary *Amber!*"

Mary Amber, trying not to hear, had caught her name, heard the sound in his voice like to the little chick that calls its mother when the hawk appears; and suddenly her fear vanished. She turned, and walked with steady step and bright eyes straight into the spare bedroom, a smile upon her lips and a rose upon her cheek that needed no cosmetics to enhance its beauty.

"Did you call me—Lyman?" she said, looking straight at him with rescue in her eyes.

He put out his hand to her, and she went and stood by the bed over across from the visitor, who had turned and was staring amazedly, insolently at her now.

Lyman Gage put out his big, wasted hand, and gathered Mary Amber's hand in his, and *she let him!*

"Mary," said Lyman Gage possessively, and there were both boldness and appeal in his eyes as he looked at her, "I want Miss Harrower to know you; Miss Amber, Miss Harrower."

Elinore Harrower had risen with one hand on the back of her chair; and her crimson lips parted, a startled expression in her eyes. Her rich furs had fallen back, and revealed a rich and vampish little frock beneath; but she was not thinking of her frock just then. She was looking from one to the other of the two before her.

"I don't understand!" she said haughtily. "Did you know her before?"

Lyman Gage flashed a look at Mary for indulgence, and answered happily.

"Our friendship dates back to when we were children and I spent a summer with my Aunt Marilla teasing Mary, and letting the sawdust out of her dolls." He gave a daring glance at Mary, and found the twinkles in her eyes playing with the dimples at the corner of her mouth; and his fingers clung more warmly around hers.

The two were so absorbedly interested in this little comedy they were enacting that they had quite failed to notice its effect upon the audience. Elinore Harrower had gathered her fur robes about her, and was fastening

them proudly at her throat. Her dark
eyes were two points of steel, and the
little white teeth that bit into the pout-
ing crimson under lip looked vicious
and suggestive.

"I did not understand," said Elinore
haughtily. "I thought you were among
strangers, and needed some one. I will
leave you to your friends. You always
did like simple country ways, I remember;" and she cast a withering
glance around.

"Why, where is Aunt Rilla, Mary?"
asked Lyman, innocently ignoring the
sneer of his guest. "Aunt Marilla!"
he raised his voice, looking toward the
door. "Aunt Marilla, won't you please
come here?"

Miss Marilla, her heart a perfect
tumult of joy to hear him call her that
way, straightened up from her ambush
outside the door, and entered precipi-
tately, just as the haughty guest was

about to stalk from the room, if one so small and exquisite as Elinore can be said to stalk. The result was a collision that quite spoiled the effect of the exit, and the two ladies looked at each other for a brief instant much as two cats might have done under similar circumstances.

Mary Amber's eyes were dancing, and Lyman Gage wanted to laugh, but he controlled his voice.

"Aunt Marilla, this is Miss Harrower, a girl who used to be an old friend of mine, and she thinks she can't stay any longer. Would you mind taking her down to the door? Good-by, Elinore. Congratulations! And I hope you'll be very happy!" He held out his free hand—the other still held Mary Amber's, and the smile upon his lips was full of merriment. But Elinore Harrower ignored the hand and the congratulations; and, drawing her fur

mantle once more about her small
haughty shoulders, she sailed from the
room, her coral and silver toque held
high, and her little red mouth drooping
with scorn and defeat. Miss Marilla,
all hospitality now that she understood,
offered tea and cake, but was vouch-
safed no answer whatever; and so in
joyous, wondering silence she attended
her soldier's guest to the door.

Lyman Gage lay back on his pillows,
his face turned away from Mary Amber,
listening; but his hand still held Mary
Amber's. And Mary Amber, standing
quietly by his side, listening too,
seemed to understand that the curtain
had not fallen yet, not quite, upon the
little play; for a smile wove in and out
among the dimples near her lips, and her
eyes were dancing little happy lights of
mirth. It was not until the front door
shut upon the guest and they heard the
motor's soft purr as the car left the

house that they felt the tenseness of the moment relax, and consciousness of their position stole upon them.

"Mary, Mary Amber!" whispered Lyman Gage softly, looking up into her face, "can you ever forgive me for all this?"

He held her hand, and his eyes pleaded for him.

"But it is all true. There *is* another one. *I love you!* And oh, I'm so tired. Mary Amber, can you forgive me—and —and love me, just a little bit?"

Down upon her knees went Mary Amber beside that bed, and gathered her soldier boy within her strong young arms, drawing his tired head upon her firm, sweet shoulder.

When Miss Marilla trotted back upstairs on her weary, glad feet, and put her head in at the door fearfully, to see how her boy had stood the strain of the visitor—and to berate herself for having allowed a stranger to come up without warning, she found them so, with Mary Amber soothing her patient to sleep by kisses on his tired eyelids, and the soldier's big white hand enfolding Mary's little one contentedly, while the man's low voice growled tenderly:

"Mary, you are the only girl I ever really loved. I didn't know there was a girl like you when I knew her."

So Miss Marilla drew the door to softly lest Molly Poke should come snooping round that way, and trotted off to the kitchen to see about some charlotte russe for supper, a great thankful gladness growing in her heart, for—oh! suppose it had been that other—hussy!

THE END